Rosa the Alligator

World Writing in French
A Winthrop-King Institute Series

Series Editors
Charles Forsdick (University of Liverpool)
and
Martin Munro (Florida State University)

Advisory Board Members
Jennifer Boum Make (Georgetown University)
Michelle Bumatay (Florida State University)
William Cloonan (Florida State University)
Michaël Ferrier (Chuo University)
Michaela Hulstyn (Stanford Univesity)
Khalid Lyamlahy (University of Chicago)
Helen Vassallo (University of Exeter)

There is a growing interest among Anglophone readers in literature in translation, including contemporary writing in French in its richness and diversity. The aim of this new series is to publish cutting-edge contemporary French-language fiction, travel writing, essays and other prose works translated for an English-speaking audience. Works selected will reflect the diversity, dynamism, originality, and relevance of new and recent writing in French from across the archipelagoes – literal and figurative – of the French-speaking world. The series will function as a vital reference point in the area of contemporary French-language prose in English translation. It will draw on the expertise of its editors and advisory board to seek out and make available for English-language readers a broad range of exciting new work originally published in French. This series is published in partnership with the Winthrop-King Institute, Florida State University.

Marie-Célie Agnant

Rosa the Alligator

Translated by Amy B. Reid
Introduction by Joëlle Vitiello

Liverpool University Press

First published in English translation by Liverpool University Press 2025
Liverpool University Press
4 Cambridge Street
Liverpool
L69 7ZU

Rosa the Alligator was first published in French as *Un alligator nommé Rosa*
© Marie-Célie Agnant & les Éditions du remue-ménage, 2007

English translation copyright © Amy B. Reid, 2025

The right of Marie-Célie Agnant to be identified as the author of this work and
Amy B. Reid to be identified as translator of this work has been asserted by them
in accordance with the Copyright, Designs and Patents Act 1988.

British Library Cataloguing-in-Publication data
A British Library CIP record is available

ISBN 978-1-83553-967-5 hardback
ISBN 978-1-83553-968-2 paperback
ISBN 978-1-83553-969-9 epdf
ISBN 978-1-83553-970-5 epub

Typeset by Carnegie Book Production, Lancaster

In Lieu of Acknowledgments ...

We are not all born equal ...

Some of us are born of fathers unknown, others are so lucky to have more than one.

I have the good fortune of being among the latter. I dedicate this book to their memory: Clerveau Rateau, a well-known lawyer during his life, one of the first victims of the Duvalierist terror, disappeared in the dungeons of the regime ... I was barely three years old when Duvalier came to power. Despite everything, the nights when fear drowns out existence remain present within me, faces melting into tragic masks, a house petrified, anguish, waiting ... A father comes out of hiding to see his children. Hot on his tail, Barbot's troops and others of their ilk. A good man, as one said back in the day—a time that has passed and will not return. This country of unmemory has fallen so low ... There are some victims who have managed to drown everything in forgetfulness, even the taste of the abundant tears they shed ...

I dedicate this book also to my second father, Albert Dominique. The father who raised me, whom I saw leave the house each morning in his immaculate white shirt, looking for our daily bread. He seemed out of place in this world. *Papa gâteau*, a bit of a poet, a bit mad, yes, for sure ... He loved to sing and recite poetry, he loved books. I would swipe them from him to read in secret. He'd threaten me, telling me that I'd spend the rest of my life selling papers or second-hand stuff whenever I fell asleep on top of my schoolwork or just got lost in a dream. He'd make me repeat this phrase written on the blackboard: "Célie will be a woman of letters." May his wishes be completely fulfilled. He left us too soon, too soon for me. My first encounter with death and the despair born of that loss, the absence of someone who will not return. He, too, was a victim of the incessant visits of the *Macoutes* and Duvalier's torturers to the house. In the end, when he was already fairly old, he opted for exile. At least we know where his bones lie.

And the third one, my biological father. He had a booming voice, loved to write, and hated Duvalier. Like a kite racing after the clouds, he chased women, made babies, was revered by them all, Joseph Agnant. Today, I've settled my score with him, because despite his contradictions, he gave me, according to my mother, the most precious of gifts: the hatred of *macoutisme*, of everything connected to it, and an unconditional love of justice. An unhappy man, no doubt. In this country where the word "justice" was long ago crossed off all vocabulary lists, where might makes right, he soon folded up his robes, put away his books, and left, taking with him his dreams for the country and for all the noble causes to defend.

This book is just a work of fiction, and no fiction can presume to accurately depict the scope of the Duvalierist horror. Still, I read certain books, and also searched the archives—those of the *Centre international de documentation et d'information haïtienne* [International Center for Documentation and Information about Haiti] or CIDHICA, in Montreal, where I discovered, along with many photos of the time, which inspired me, newspaper accounts of murders and executions and Duvalier's horrifying speeches, written by learned people who put their knowledge to his service. I thank the Center's team for putting all those materials at my disposal. I would like to express my thanks to all my many relatives and friends who encouraged me, gave me their constant support so that I could make headway with my writing. To Benjamin Saint-Dic and Serge Rousseau, who read the first draft: my thanks to Ben for his indulgence, and to Serge for his implacable severity. All of my gratitude to Rose-Flore Bélizaire, who so generously gave me her time, for our long and fruitful conversations about this era that so profoundly marked us both. To my editors, Rachel Bédard, Élise Bergeron, Ginette Péloquin, and Catherine Germain, who continue to believe in me and who continually, patiently, and firmly, send me back to my half-finished texts.

Marie-Célie Agnant
Montreal, 2007

Contents

Introduction

Amy Reid's translation of *Un alligator nommé Rosa*, the third of Marie-Célie Agnant's novels, represents a significant addition to her body of work in English. Agnant is a novelist, poet, storyteller, educator, translator, and activist, who has lived in Montreal since the 1970s. To date she has published four major novels, two volumes of short stories, three collections of poetry, four novels for youth, three volumes of tales for young audiences, and countless texts published in magazines and anthologies; her work has been widely translated into English, Portuguese, German, Korean, Japanese, Spanish, Dutch, and Italian. Agnant has received several literary distinctions and was a finalist for two major Quebec prizes. Her first novel, *La Dot de Sara* (1995), has had three editions in Quebec. Widely studied in schools, colleges, and universities in Quebec, but also in advanced French classes in Canada and the United States, it has become a classic in courses about Haitian Literature and Haitian Studies and in courses on immigration. The novel was reissued in 2022 in a bilingual French/Creole edition, translated into Creole by Agnant herself. Agnant's second novel, *Le livre d'Emma* (2001), about the long-term effect of slavery on Afro-descendants, has been equally well received and is studied in various settings; a complex narrative about different modes of writing and speaking, of narrating individual and collective memory, it garnered the attention of scholars all over the world. It has been translated into Catalan, Spanish, Italian, and English. Agnant's most recent novel, *Femmes au temps des carnassiers* (2015), is also a novel about justice, about restoring the voice of a feminist journalist violently attacked by the macoutist regime of François Duvalier. The novel was translated into English in Canada under the title *A Knife In the Sky* (2023). Marie-Célie Agnant has also published articles in Creole for the feminist journal *AyitiFanm*, directed by long-time feminist friend, Clorinde Zephir.[1] In 2023, Agnant was appointed Canadian Parliamentary Poet Laureate, a position she resigned from in October 2023 to remain faithful to her convictions and beliefs in social justice and in a better world.

A quick bibliographic search shows that hundreds of articles, book chapters, and dissertations in various languages examine Agnant's work. In 2013, a book of essays exploring the role of memory in her writing, *Paroles et silences chez Marie-Célie Agnant: L'oublieuse mémoire d'Haïti*, was published by Karthala. Memory is definitely at work in *Rosa the Alligator*. The novel, first published in 2007, taps directly into the author's memory of the terror the Duvalier regime unleashed on Haitian citizens. Her experience as a witness of some of the most violent repressions by the agents of François Duvalier is a thread that informs much of her work, from the powerful stories in the collection *Le Silence comme le sang* (1997) through *A Knife in the Sky* and, of course, *Rosa the Alligator*.

Rosa the Alligator was written twenty years after the fall of Baby Doc, François Duvalier's son, nearly forty-five years after the massacres of April 26, 1963, when the dictator took revenge on the families he suspected of having abducted his children, and of June 1964, when he eliminated a group of freedom fighters who had come back from exile to free their nation of his rule. Agnant often mentions that the generations who lived and suffered under the Duvalier regime were "baîllonées," silenced. Her writing sets out to open up speech and emotions, to render visible the indelible traces that the period of impunity—which lasted over a full generation, from 1957 to 1986—left on the memories and souls of those who were not allowed to mourn their loved ones who disappeared in the jails of Fort Dimanche, at the hands of torturers like "Madame Rosa," in the ravines of the countryside, or in the mud fields of Titanyen, the mass graves on the northern outskirts of Port-au-Prince that she describes so vividly in her short story, "Le Silence comme le sang," and where many of the victims of the January 12, 2010 earthquake are now buried. Despite some courageous attempts to hold a trial after the return of Jean-Claude Duvalier in 2011, justice was not done. The nineteen witnesses who survived the horrors of the repression and courageously testified

---

1 See Joëlle Vitiello, "Le bruit des femmes: écrivaines et militantes." https://diginole.lib.fsu.edu/islandora/object/fsu%3A722937.

about the deaths that occurred in the infamous jails of the regime were denied justice, as Jean-Claude Duvalier passed away from a heart attack before the end of his trial.[2] Thus, the past continues to haunt the present. No commission on truth and justice or truth and reconciliation about the Duvalier period ever took place in Haiti,[3] not even after the first commemorations of the April 26 massacre, which were held in 2013, fifty years after the fact. Liberating the silenced voices of Haiti's past from the forgetfulness of history, *Rosa the Alligator* centers them in her readers' field of vision in very astute ways, and provides, if not justice, stories where a form of justice is served. How so?

The novel brings together three characters in a plot that explores trauma, revenge, and justice. Antoine is a survivor of the Duvalier regime. As a child, he saw his entire family assassinated by agents of the regime, including a woman, Rosa Bosquet. The tragedy that traumatized Antoine is based on real events, and Rosa Bosquet is based on a real woman executioner, Madame Max Adolphe, who was close to François Duvalier. Antoine arrives in a small fictional village in the South of France, Gourdaix, where he has located the executioner of his family. He manages to get hired as an aide to the woman, now old and very sick, who cannot move and who refuses to speak to him. Rosa's "niece," Laura, herself a victim of the regime, was adopted and raised by her parents' tormentor. Together, Antoine and Laura confront the past of the dictatorship and debate whether justice can be done, should be done, or whether they will always be prisoners of history and of their memories. The novel is divided into two parts, Antoine's story, and the consequences of his irruption in Laura and Rosa's life.

The novel explores the deep ways in which the unaddressed past continues to haunt the present of victims and executioners alike, albeit in different forms. Through the eyes of two victims of the

---

2 See "'The Baby Doc' Duvalier Prosecution," The Center for Justice and Accountability. https://cja.org/what-we-do/litigation/amicus-briefs/the-baby-doc-duvalier-prosecution/.

3 The only Haitian National Truth and Justice Commission was formed to identify the many human rights violations perpetrated by the military junta that ousted President Jean-Bertrand Aristide in 1991. It culminated in a report, *Si m pa rele* (1998). https://ufdc.ufl.edu/UF00085926/00001/images.

regime, Antoine and Laura, and its executioner, Rosa Bosquet, the novel revisits one of the most horrible instances of violent repression by the dictatorship, when, after two of his children were kidnapped and held for one day, the president and his army of *Macoutes* went on a killing rampage in the capital to punish potential accomplices. They burned down houses with entire families inside. The repression became part of the nation's collective (traumatic) memory. In the novel, this episode is narrated in fragments through the memory of Antoine, who was a child at the time. The author also focuses on the acts of a female executioner. The real Rosalie Bosquet was an officer in Duvalier's paramilitary death squads, known as the *Tontons Macoutes*. She headed and trained the *Fillettes Lalo*, cohorts of young women who joined and trained the paramilitary squads. In this way, Agnant introduces a gender component that has often been overlooked in historical accounts and examines the role of women, both as victims with Laura and as executioners with Rosa.[4] The novel, by addressing crimes committed under Papa Doc's regime, confronts the past from the perspective of the present: how can the victims move forward, forget, forgive? How can they free themselves of their ongoing trauma? I have suggested elsewhere that Agnant's writing embodies "une écriture citoyenne," that is, a writing concerned with justice and solidarity, that raises consciousness in its wake and makes audible the voices of the silenced.[5] Similarly, in his essay, "La rage retenue de Marie-Célie Agnant," Thomas Spear ponders whether the novel itself has a role to play in the search for justice, as a form of symbolic reparation that, nonetheless, restores the humanity of the victims and does not let the culprits get away.[6]

---

4   The exhibit "OppresSOEURS/Opprimées: femmes haïtiennes durant la dictature duvaliériste (1957–1986)" at the Webster Library of Concordia University in Montreal in April 2013, and later accessible as a virtual exhibit, was exceptional for its focus on Haitian women as both victims and active participants in the dictatorship.

5   Joëlle Vitiello, "La mémoire dans les romans et nouvelles de Marie-Célie Agnant," in Colette Boucher and Thomas C. Spear, eds. *Paroles et silences chez Marie-Célie Agnant: L'oublieuse mémoire d'Haïti* (Paris: Karthala, 2013), p. 160.

6   Thomas C. Spear, "La rage retenue de Marie-Célie Agnant," in Boucher and Spear, *Paroles et silences chez Marie-Célie Agnant*, p. 153.

The literary and esthetic significance of the work is also multiple: (a) instead of taking place in Haiti, the novel unfolds in a small village of Provence, in a beautiful touristic setting that Agnant captures well. While this reminds readers that France welcomed the fleeing family of the dictator and his acolytes, the shift also provides a displaced and reflective frame for the exploration of the traumatic history of Haiti under the Duvaliers; (b) the novel evolves through the interior journey of a long-time victim of the regime, whose life was defined by the murder of his family. The novel takes us through the various emotional states the main character, Antoine, experiences in his quest for justice; (c) just as the dictatorship exists as a ghost that haunts the novel, the executioner, Rosa, is a spectral, silenced presence; unable or unwilling to speak, she wants to write her memoirs but loses control of the narrative when Antoine becomes her ghostwriter. So as to exorcize Haiti's demons, Agnant makes a clear choice to give voice to the victims and not to the torturer. The novel is a tour de force for how effectively it tells a story of Haiti outside Haiti, weaving history into a tale that at once represents and reverses the historical silence of the regime's victims, enfolding several generations and excavating multiple layers of crimes against Haitians, notably the kidnapping and training of children to serve the regime. For readers, the work has far-reaching implications, as Agnant's powerful, innovative voice provides an invitation to a philosophical and ethical reflection on how best to attain justice.

Few contemporary writers have as clear a view and as courageous a position as Agnant does when it comes to the Duvalier dictatorship, and to impunity in general. If Haitian novelists grappled with the regime's history in the 1970s and 1980s (Émile Ollivier and Gérard Étienne, who also wrote in Canada, for instance), it is not the primary focus of contemporary Haitian literature written in French. In that light, it is important to note that Agnant's *Un Alligator nommé Rosa* is the first of several recent books that do address the dictatorship, all written by Haitian women writers. Agnant's book was published in 2007. *La Mémoire aux abois* (*Memory at Bay*), by Evelyne Trouillot, and *Saisons sauvages* (*Savage Seasons*), by Kettly Mars, which also address the dictatorship, memory, and history, were both published in 2010, and Jan J. Dominique's *L'Echo de leurs voix* was published in 2016. Each book confronts the legacy of the dictatorship in its own distinct way, from a reconciliatory approach

(Trouillot) to the recognition of widespread complicity with the regime (Mars) and the examination of how Haiti's history and some of its irreconcilable memories can be transmitted to younger generations in the Canadian diaspora (Dominique).

The fact that *Un Alligator nommé Rosa* is the first of these recent books to address this legacy is significant precisely because of the ethical ground on which Agnant stands. This English translation will allow non-francophone readers who have read Trouillot's and Mars's novels in English to have a new perspective on the history and long-term traumatic effects of the dictatorship. For that matter, while they are not the first ones to have written about the encounters of victims and executioners—Edwige Danticat in *The Dew Breaker*, Étienne in *Un Ambassadeur Macoute à Montréal*, and *Haitian Corner*, by filmmaker Raoul Peck, all come to mind—this quartet of writers focuses on one slice of Haitian history, but to very different ends, depending on how their characters negotiate the weight of the past. Marie-Célie Agnant's novel demonstrates that Agnant is and can only be on the side of justice. One of the many benefits of the publication of this translation now is that it invites younger generations of readers with Haitian ancestry, especially those from the Haitian diaspora who grew up with English as their first language, to grapple with the ethical complexity of Haitian history. For a general readership, the questions raised by Agnant's characters go beyond the specific situation of Haiti: when facing the legacies of human rights crimes, how should societies react? What would a fair reparation be like? How can we move forward without first confronting the past? Without first recognizing and confronting history? Whose voices do we need to hear? Those are issues that remain current, so *Rosa the Alligator* will resonate with many anglophone readers not only from the United States but from elsewhere because the questions raised by Antoine and Laura have a universal quality. When a victim has the opportunity to become the executioner, what does it mean to be just, ethical, moral? The book will no doubt provoke fascinating discussions around the dinner table or in classrooms.

This introduction would not be complete without a few words about the translation itself and its creator. If the original novel is a tour de force that provides many modes of narration, with dialogues and interior monologues, fragments of writing, fragments of memory, and fragments of history, the translation is also a tour de force. Amy Reid is an experienced translator, having worked with multiple authors from Sub-Saharan Africa, including Cameroonian writer Patrice Nganang, and her expertise allowed her to navigate challenging passages in the book. Her dedication to seeing the book through has been admirable and it is a pleasure to read. Join us.

Joëlle Vitiello
St. Paul, Minnesota

Translator's Foreword

As a translator and professor of French, I spend a lot of time wrestling with language, trying to find the right words to say what I mean and, what's both harder and more rewarding, the right words to say what someone else means. Many of the novels I have translated are explicitly about language—working at the interstices between different languages and idioms to challenge our understandings of past and present. And yet, this translation—a project interrupted by the pandemic—has pushed me to think differently about what's at stake ethically in the representation of language.

As a storyteller, novelist, and poet, Marie-Célie Agnant has a virtuosic way with words. But in *Un Alligator nommé Rosa*, she plumbs the limits of language, asking weighty questions about what comes of telling the truth about historical events many would prefer to leave buried, and about our responsibilities to other people's voices. We see and hear in this novel how Antoine and Laura suffer because of the stories they bear, how language fails them at crucial moments, and how words ultimately help them to find their way through. We also see and hear how Antoine, in particular, finds comfort in his wordless interactions with the natural world, a sign of Agnant's hope for our future. But all voices are not equal, and Agnant makes a clear ethical choice not to give the floor to apologists of state-sanctioned brutality, whether in Duvalier's Haiti or anywhere else. Because Rosa shows no remorse, she is never allowed to justify her actions but can only bray and bellow. That's a harsh choice, out of sync with our traditions of legal justice, perhaps, but Agnant assumes her responsibility for it, reminding us that there are not always two sides to a story—and that we are responsible for which voices we do and do not hear.

I offer my sincere and heartfelt thanks to Marie-Célie Agnant for her courage as a writer, the trust she placed in me as a translator, her generosity of spirit, and her friendship. Un très grand merci, as well, to Joëlle Vitiello, who suggested I translate this novel, who read and discussed my many drafts, and who penned the informative introduction I hope you've just read. Without her dedication and support, this project would not have come to be. It was my good fortune that Martin Munro and Charles Forsdick announced the Florida State University/Liverpool University Press translation series, World Writing in French: New Archipelagoes, in late fall 2023; it's an honor to work with them and the editorial team to inaugurate it. Literature is an act of faith and optimism—if we create books, people will read them—and I thank everyone involved in this project for helping to make significant works of fiction, like Agnant's *Rosa the Alligator*, available to more readers.

On a personal note, I could not have completed this project were it not for the support of my family and friends. To my kids, Jacob, Miriam and Ben, and our dog (who is named Rosa but shares no other traits with the Alligator), know that I love you "more than I can say." I worked on this translation while on research leave from New College of Florida, where I had the distinct privilege of teaching for almost thirty years. My appreciation for my colleagues and students, past and present, is immense. Over the past two years, I have been buoyed up in more ways that I can express by the creativity, fierceness, and compassion of the Novo community. I'll say no more—but trust that those who have ridden out the storms with me understand ... *Onè, respè.*

Amy B. Reid
Sarasota, Florida

Rosa the Alligator

By Marie-Célie Agnant

Translated by Amy B. Reid

To Guy Roumer,
Since we are, first of all,
only men and women ...
absolutely imperfect ...
human beings in the process of becoming

I will go down to Hades and shine there among the dead.

Homer, *The Iliad*

Part I

1

With heavy steps, the man climbs the small set of stairs and bends over to set an enormous suitcase down on the ground. He hesitates before placing his hand on the door latch. That's when she feels his presence. Through the pane of glass, she notices his fingers, long and thin. She sees his lips moving, but hears nothing of what he says. The brutal light of a bare bulb on the wall illuminates his face. He seems a bit anxious. Disregarding her aunt's directive that once the latch has been drawn no one may cross the threshold of the bistro, she pulls the keys from the pocket of her apron and opens the door.

With his back slightly stooped and holding his hat in his hands, he pauses in the doorway, as if, at the last moment, he might change his mind. Then he picks up the suitcase again, pushes open the door with one foot, and carefully sets his luggage down inside. She looks him over, eyeing critically his hands nervously fidgeting with his beret. He awkwardly folds the beret and stuffs it into a pocket. He takes several steps, looks around the room. She hears him say two very simple words: "Nice place!" And, without fully understanding why—though clearly because of those two words— she feels herself carried away by a whirlwind of anger, despite all her efforts to contain it. Just as she is about to let him have it, he quickly turns to face her.

"I've been sent by the agency," he announces.

"I'd started to worry."

Her tone leaves no doubt about her displeasure.

"Please forgive me."

He bows slightly before continuing.

"I climbed the hill as fast as I could, I was panicked at the idea of finding the doors locked. Now it's simple, I almost feel like a happy man!"

"Good for you!"

Unsettled by her aggressive tone, the man gestures towards his bags, trying to express his embarrassment.

"Just think ... if I had to leave and find somewhere to stay for the night ..."

"So, you are Monsieur Antoine Guibert?"

He notes the impatience in her voice and answers with a nod. Then, as if to confirm his identity, he steps forward and offers his hand, a handshake he hopes is solid and confident. Despite her bad mood, she appreciates this broad palm, warm and enveloping, that literally swallows up her own, so small and chubby. But since she just stands there, staring at him and not saying a word, he bends down, clearly uncomfortable, and tentatively places a hand on the suitcase.

"It's already quite late, that's true. But I just missed the previous bus. I am really so sorry ..."

He stands back up, slowly unfolding his frail frame, and stammers out, unconvincingly:

"If you'd rather, for tonight ... I can try, with your help ... to find some little inn nearby."

"Not at all, not at all."

Walking quickly, she heads to the entrance, relocks the door, and then slips the key ring back into her pocket.

"You see ..." she begins, clearly trying to make up for her rather glacial welcome, "I'd given up on you! Communication with the agency has been difficult. They'd promised to confirm your arrival ahead of time ..."

With a wave, she points to a clock whose arms give the time: 11 p.m.

"I was sure you wouldn't make it today."

"Were you getting ready to leave?"

Instead of answering, she goes to the windows, draws the curtains, and turns off the lights. The entranceway is plunged into a darkness that seems to her deeper than usual.

Antoine pretends not to notice the bitterness of her tone and replies enthusiastically.

"I promise, I'd sleep like a rock right there on that table. Believe me, I'm used to sleeping when and wherever I can."

He watches the woman out of the corner of his eye, wondering how long she's going to go back and forth like this, shifting from rudeness to affability. She shrugs her shoulders, as if signaling her desire to put an end to the conversation.

"Let me finish setting up here. That way I'll be a few steps ahead tomorrow."

"There's no hurry. According the agency's instructions, I don't start work until 4 p.m., so I have all day to rest. Can I help you?"

Without giving her time to refuse, he quickly picks up a tablecloth and folds it in quarters with one fluid motion. He moves deftly from one table to the next, checking each tablecloth, removing those that are dirty. For a short moment, she watches him, then picks up a stack of clean tablecloths and, following his trail, starts covering the bare tables.

"I've got to say," the man begins, as he approaches the last table in the back of the room, "you're really in the middle of nowhere here. If I were in Bar-sur-Loup or even Bousquet, I'd never think of coming up here for a meal … unless," he adds, glancing at her with a smile in his eyes, "you have some specialty found nowhere else!"

"You got it! That's what draws the clients."

Bitterly, she adds:

"That's just how people are, aren't they? Never satisfied with what they have on hand, they go looking elsewhere."

He notes the muted rage of her gestures as she smooths the tablecloths with swift, brusque moves and places at the center of each table a porcelain vase, which she'll surely fill with fresh cut flowers tomorrow. From time to time, she glances at the entrance. Curious, he hazards a guess:

"Are you waiting for someone?"

Like a child caught red-handed, her eyes snap open wide. She quickly turns away and stammers:

"No … no … no one … really. I'm not expecting anyone … It's an old habit," she finally admits, trying to control her voice. "My aunt used to drop by some evenings, suddenly appearing when I least expected her. Since her last attack, she doesn't come here anymore. But I still feel like she could show up at any moment."

Quickly changing the topic, she asks:

"Did the agency give you details about your lodging?"

He opens his mouth, but she just keeps going.

"It's in a new villa that's been built, attached to the main house by a walkway. But you don't need to worry, because my aunt is bedridden … that's the term you use for paralysis in the medical field, right? It doesn't matter if she's right nearby, she can't hurt you, don't worry."

As soon as she says those last words, the young woman bites her lip so hard she flinches. She's already said too much. "Just what do I know, really, about this person I'm welcoming in like an old friend? Am I that hungry for friendship and attention? 'What a bad habit!' as Rosa would've said." Then she remembers that she's not alone. The man waits patiently beside her, as polite as can be. Suddenly exasperated, the woman looks once more around the dining room and says:

"Come on! We're going!"

Dumbstruck, he follows her silently. She opens and then locks the door behind them. They go down the steps, start off along the path. He trails along, dragging his feet slightly because of his enormous suitcase; he can already feel his fingers tingling. His arm is getting heavy. He should have hoisted the suitcase up onto his shoulders, but it's too late now. He'd like to talk to her, to say something, anything, but not knowing what or how, he hesitates.

"You … uh, you live here?"

He stumbles over the syllables, then adds:

"You live with your aunt?"

"No!"

That "no," more cutting than the lash of a whip, is just too much.

"I'm not trying to be indiscreet, but it's normal for me to ask some questions. They were really short on details at the agency."

"Please forgive my impatience. Not living under the same roof as my aunt in no way frees me from my obligations to her, and that irritates me. She is a huge weight on my shoulders."

She says all of that quickly, in one breath, then adds, more softly:

"Me, I live at the edge of town, a little house surrounded by old cork trees and maritime pines, just at the bottom of the hill. With its blue shutters, you can't miss it from the road. My house is my refuge. I could never live under the same roof as my aunt, never again!" she snaps.

In the growing dark, he senses more than sees her bitterness, her face twisted with anger.

"In fact," she goes on, "only the night nurse stays in the house, and, as of tomorrow, that will be you. Unless you decide to turn tail and run. It's already happened, you know!"

He can't see her face, but he could swear she lifted her eyes to weigh the effect of her words on him. He suspects that she'd like to hear him say he wants to leave right then and there. But that's because she doesn't know the real reason he's come. She knows nothing of the duty he cannot shirk. He reflexively turns his head toward her, but all he hears is the sound of her breath, coming short and fast.

"I'm surprised to learn that nurses don't like it here," he forces himself to say, just to break the silence, which is as uncomfortable as the hefty suitcase he's trundling along. "The area is wonderful. Between sea and mountain. Who could ask for more?"

"Not everyone knows how to appreciate beauty! As for me, I just try to make sure things are clear, because I don't like people to feel like they've been ambushed. So, I try to give the best description I can of the situation. Without exaggerating, I can assure you that my aunt does nothing at all to make herself agreeable or to keep on those hired to care for her."

Her voice begins to crack, but he can't tell if it's from anger, worry, or fear.

A solid wall surrounds the property. Built of enormous, rough stones, it's coiffed with an abundance of leafy vine. The ivy grabs ahold of the stones, leaping with wild abandon from the ground up to the crenellations, taking the cornices by assault. Camouflaged in this way, the dwelling to which she is leading him is invisible from the outside. You can feel it there in the shadows, imposing and mysterious. The gleam of the floodlights only emphasizes the surrounding darkness, which swallows up the hill on which the house is perched. A bouquet of scents, a heady mix of wild thyme and rosemary, greets them. They hear the sharp barks of a dog.

They pass by the majestic entrance and head along the east side, toward a sort of greenhouse filled with all sorts of rare plants. Impressive, he thinks, looking all around. He pauses to gaze at the somber mass of the house, trying to find the right adjective for that impenetrable citadel.

In contrast, the villa where he will stay is a new building, with fine, clean lines, a much more reassuring style, to his mind. It connects to the main house through the greenhouse, which is also bathed in a blinding glow from the floodlights fixed on the wall. As they circle back around to the entrance, the man remarks:

"Just one of those bulbs would be enough to light up that greenhouse."

"You're absolutely right. My aunt is terrified of darkness. She even needs a nightlight in her bedroom."

As if sharing a secret, the man continues:

"For a long time, I felt an almost irrational fear of the dark. When I was a child, I'd sometimes spend the whole night curled up in a ball beneath the covers. I was so afraid that something would come out of the dark and pounce on me, tear me out of my bed and carry me away."

Those words, that voice, brought back her own night terrors, all those faceless, unnamed dangers that haunted her childhood and adolescence. And the immense solitude born of that fear. Instinctively, she holds her head up high and declares, her voice unexpectedly certain:

"Sadly, there is no remedy for our fear!"

She hurries on, muttering to herself, "Let's get this over and done with."

Antoine gazes happily at the bay windows, large pools where the sun can stream in. His eyes are drawn to a series of stoneware pots attached to a metal railing around a narrow terrace along the right side of the villa. Painted in bright colors, with Aztec motifs, the pots hold plants with wilted stems and faded leaves, crying out their burning thirst. She notices the sad look in his eyes at the sight of the neglected plants and feels she has to explain, come up with an excuse.

"The cleaning woman is supposed to water them. How many times did I ask her to! With her, you really have to repeat the same things again and again."

"Tomorrow, I'll take care of the plants," Antoine promises.

He picks up one of the leaves scattered on the ground and caresses it, rubbing its smooth edge with his finger. The woman leans against the rough wall, clearly in no hurry to go into the villa. He listens carefully to what she says, certain that she is holding back, that she'd like to say more, that she's just waiting for a sign, the right question. Forgetting her determination to keep her distance, she starts to speak, again spitting out her words in exasperation.

"In any case, she can't even get out of bed anymore. She's entirely dependent on her caretakers. From now on, all she can do is write, writing day and night in her damned notebooks! No matter that she complains about how her swollen fingers ache, she has got it into her head that she's going to write her memoirs."

"I know. I was hired in part to help her complete her work. You should know that; it's in the contract."

"Of course. I just want to be sure that they informed you of that absurd requirement."

"Unlike you, I'm really excited about that project, especially since she insists we work on it through the night. Otherwise, I wouldn't be here. The idea is original, just like your aunt's character, or so it seems to me. And then, writing is one of the most effective therapies."

"If you want my opinion, I think it's ridiculous. Pretentious and ridiculous!"

She tosses out that phrase as if she were throwing a knife; then, as her fingers fumble through the tangle of keys on the ring, she mumbles impatiently:

"It doesn't matter if I have all the keys, I can never get in anywhere! Such a bad habit—to hold on to useless keys. I can't tell one from the other."

She examines each of the keys and tries them all, one after the other. After several vain attempts, one last key squeaks and turns in the lock. She opens the door and immediately a bright light bursts forth. Antoine looks in and sees a huge living room with very high ceilings.

"Another of Aunt Rosa's ideas," she explains, her voice still sounding just as aggravated. "The lights turn on everywhere here, as soon as you open the door."

Moving quickly, she paces back and forth, going through her list.

"This couch turns into a bed, for guests. But we are so far from everything, who would ever come all the way up here? Unless you have very devoted friends who stop by now and again to keep you company. Only a few tourists, either lost or looking for solitude, venture into the area. The truck drivers are my most faithful customers. Otherwise, there are just a few old folks who come around on organized bus tours.

The woman's voice has risen into a sharp whine. Caught up in the wave of emotion that washes over him as he finally steps into the villa, Antoine barely hears her. Yet he follows her across the main room, step by step, as if obeying an order.

Suddenly, she pushes up her sleeve, checks her watch, and, in a panic, exclaims:

"What a chatterbox I am! It's almost one in the morning."

"I didn't notice how time had flown," the man replies, apologetically. "We can go over all this tomorrow, if you'd rather. Just leave me the key. I can give you a call tomorrow at the bistro. What time will you be there?"

"Around 10 a.m. But, wait ..."

Instead of handing him the keys, she heads down the hallway.

"I have to show you the bedroom, where to find sheets and blankets. The nights here are often chilly."

He follows her, thinking all the while that, just like him, she must fear the solitude of her bedroom, where all she has for company are her own wild thoughts and the fears she struggles to keep at bay. He hurries after her, tries to convince her that a simple bed is enough for him, but she is determined to rush around the house, anxiously looking at her watch all the while. At the far end of the hall, in front of a double door, she stops. The bedroom, she announces. She moves to the side to let him go ahead.

"The bedding is stored in the cupboard; extra pillows, too."

She seems to forget that she was about to leave, so he says something, anything, just to keep the conversation going.

"Um, uh, how old is your aunt?"

"She just turned seventy-two. Were it not for the paralysis in her legs and, most of all, her obesity, she'd be quicker on her feet than either of us. You should have met her before her accident. Here!"

She hands him a key, pulled from the bunch on the ring.

"Tomorrow I'll come by to go over some other little details. I'll get here around three o'clock and then go with you to Rosa's."

"Thank you ... miss, um ..."

He realizes right then that she never actually introduced herself. She holds out her hand.

"Laura. My name is Laura. Laura Bosquet."

"It's already quite late, Laura," he begins. "Wouldn't it be better for you to sleep at your aunt's, instead of leaving in the middle of the night ..."

"Me?" she gasps, her eyes wide with panic. "Sleep at Rosa's? I'd rather die! No, I'm quite certain."

Her aggravation is clear as she stomps off, saying brusquely over her shoulder:

"Sleep well, Monsieur Guibert. I'll see you tomorrow!"

"Call me Antoine—it's much simpler," he replies.

Timidly, he adds, in a soft voice:

"I'm so sorry to have upset you. Are you sure you want to leave? It's so dark on the mountain ..."

"I'm used to it," she says with a shrug, adding quickly as she heads out, "I'm not afraid of the dark ... and I'm certainly no Little Red Riding Hood ..."

"Well, then, goodnight, Laura," he says, reluctantly. "See you tomorrow."

"Goodnight."

2

Instead of going straight to bed, Antoine settles down on the terrace and breathes in the sharp scent of the pines. Carried along on the breeze, it dissipates the other smells, spreading out like a veil, a net that catches everything up. It seems to him that, after wandering through the trees, the wind's wild breath is more of a melancholy wail. He begins to think about Laura, is filled with deep compassion for her. A sad and bitter wrinkle creases his brow as he wonders whether she hopes that her isolation on this rocky mountaintop, this Eagle's Nest, as Gourdaix is sometimes called, will bring her peace? Soon he'll need to remind her that peace and silence are no more than an illusion here; the silence is filled with a painful clamor, and the peace threatened by a plague, he murmurs. What a strange creature, Antoine muses. What sort of game is she playing? Either she talks nonstop ... clearly chattering to cover up a profound unease ... or she gets scared about some little thing, upset about a misplaced word. Still, he feels more reassured than frightened by her attempts to be brusque. He wouldn't have liked to find himself faced with a woman in the throes of despair.

Inside the big house, the little dog yips listlessly. In the distance, another mutt, with a deeper and more resonant bark, picks up the refrain. Then, silence: sinister and oppressive, like a cloister ... and the whistling of the trees. Antoine thinks about Laura in her house with the blue shutters. He hadn't noticed that house on his way up the hill. Hunched over by the weight of his immense suitcase, he saw nothing and no one, wholly consumed by his worry that all the doors would be shut tight when he arrived. He tries to imagine it, like a doll's house, with lacy curtains at the windows, pillows everywhere, and a profusion of plants.

At three in the morning, he finally decides to go into the bedroom, the one that will be his now for some time. He hopes with all his heart that it will only be for a short while. As he scans the room an expression of implacable severity appears on his face. He stretches out on the bed, appreciates the firmness of the mattress. He moves his hands over it, hitting it with his fists, then sliding his hands along its silky cover. With a quick move he strips the bed, throws the spread and the matching pillows onto the parquet floor. He inspects the sheets and pillows carefully and opens the drawers and closets one after the other.

"From now on, this room is yours. For as long as it takes!" he proclaims, his voice strangely harsh. His face and fingers contract, become those of a beast that suddenly feels the need to show its claws.

His eyes fix on the down comforter lying on the floor. How awful, how vulgar they are, those bright red peonies on the quilt! He grimaces. All these things just make him sick. If there were a fireplace in the room, he'd feel a real joy seeing them go up in flames. He moves to the windows and feels the curtains, thick, made from the same fabric as the quilt. Tomorrow at the latest, he'll make these horrors disappear. The closets and drawers reek of naphthalene; replace that with lavender and rosemary, clean everything and shove all this mess into the back of a closet. For the next hour or more he continues exploring and then finally lies down, fully dressed. But sleep eludes him. Stretched out, with his arms crossed under his neck, Antoine stares fixedly at a clock shaped like a carrousel, where four ballerinas dance, keeping time with the pendulum. The hours tick by, slower than usual.

He gets up, goes over to a bookshelf built into the wall and eyes a gorgeous edition of the *Encyclopedia Britannica*: a calfskin leather cover, embossed with red and gold. Mechanically, he picks up a volume, leafing through the pages absentmindedly before grabbing another. Smooth and fine, still stuck together, its pages never suffered the assault of impatient hands or even a reader's nonchalance. He tells himself that he should sleep, gather his strength for the coming day. But the slightest creak of the branches outside, the slightest whisper of a breeze, makes him jump. He's not easily frightened, but he's always had one real fear, a deep terror with him since childhood, that a woman in a severe uniform will suddenly appear, with dark glasses covering her face and a rifle with a bayonet in her hands: Commander Rosa Bosquet!

That image makes him start to pace frantically, back and forth across the large vestibule. Now and again, he stops, trying to imagine just what Rosa Bosquet looks like now. A little, shriveled old woman who drools and sucks on her gums? The agency's records mentioned obesity. So maybe she's a bundle of limp grey flesh, where all you can see are weepy eyes? And if ... he wonders, now really afraid, what if she's really charming, with a tender and welcoming smile? Just the thought exasperates him. And what if ... if ... rather than waiting till tomorrow, waiting for Laura, I just head over to Rosa right now? He begins to tremble and shake. "Should I? Shouldn't I?" he asks, speaking as if to another self. "No, Antoine," he answers, "you know you must not." Caught between doubts, uncertainties, and what seems like an absolute duty—the coming face-to-face with Rosa—Antoine realizes he has to put on the brakes, do whatever he can to keep a whole army of specters at bay, specters who pursue him, demanding, ordering him with a determined rage to exact a punishment befitting Rosa Bosquet's crimes. He feels within him the growing impatience of a horde of demons, huddled together in his gut and on alert, ready to leap at the least sign from him. Suddenly the bedroom is a whorl of sound and fury: the impetuous breath of a band of incubi? A burning desire for justice? He sees only one thing before his eyes, an unleashed pack of mastiffs that nothing and no one can stop. They invade Rosa's lair, pull her out of her bed, drag her off into the woods to devour her.

Through the large bay window, he sees a landscape still swathed in dark, where the silhouettes of parasol pines and sturdy oaks are braced against the wind. Suddenly, strong gusts of wind rise up, whistling all around, and those trees who stand guard all through the night seem like impassive watchmen, facing off against the innocence and severity of silence.

He finally lies back down, only to continue counting the hours. His mind is like a ramshackle windmill besieged by strong winds. So close to the goal line and his doubts return: All that hard work just to end up shutting yourself away like a dog in a kennel, tied up outside Rosa's lair! You're free to leave, don't you know that? Furious, he rails, "Free from what? Free in what way? How can I claim any kind of freedom?" Finally, he asks himself, "Just what do you think will come from this meeting, Antoine? It'd be better if you just ran away." That thought barely crosses his mind before he mounts a vigorous defense against it, calling himself pitiful, a coward.

If he is apprehensive about meeting Rosa for the first time, Antoine doesn't worry much about his exchanges with Laura, which were strange to say the least. Nothing in the young woman's attitude suggests that she suspects the motives for his presence there on the mountain. Like a pebble on a path, I am still anonymous, he figures, feeling that sense of satisfaction he gets from time to time when he convinces himself that he holds all the cards. He's relieved to see the sun rise. A warm breeze blows, despite the early hour. Does the sirocco wander all the way up to these mountains? Antoine can sense the sea in the distance. He imagines it shimmering in shades of grey and feels a dull cry well up within him. Around him, inside him, everything rocks to and fro. He is nothing but a rolling sea swell, difficult to contain, and that cry so long bottled up in his gut wants only to escape. Who can understand the pain that grows in another's body? he wonders, now speaking to the endless blue abyss that still sleeps in the distance. As if in response, the sea releases rays of sunlight from its breast that swath the treetops in a brilliant robe of iridescent blue and gold.

How had he managed to hold on to the joy he finds in nature? It always amazes him, so he's determined to make the most of his time in this part of the country. You can't criticize Rosa's choice of where she invested her dough, he says as his eyes again take in the green-covered hills. He decides to go take care of the plants, a way to pass the time. He rummages around for a while and turns up a pair of pruning shears in the back of a shed. He enthusiastically cuts back and ties up the branches, several of which had been drooping on the ground. He waters each planter, fascinated by how quickly the soil soaks it up. That same thirst is eating away at me, he murmurs; now I'm finally going to lock my eyes onto those of the monster and speak right to her. A branch in one hand, the pruning shears in the other, Antoine suddenly freezes. In the health report, did they mention deafness? Immediately dropping the shears, he rushes in to look for the documents from the agency. He dumps the contents of several envelopes onto the bed and the parquet, rifles through the papers. In anguish, he scans the pages before falling back on the bed. Thank God! She's not deaf. But, he starts again, maybe she has Alzheimer's? That would be the worst! The agency never would have omitted such information ... And besides, Laura would have told me. But what if, once I'm in front of her, I find out that she's not the one I'm looking for, but some other Rosa Bosquet?

Come on, Antoine, you're falling apart! He forces himself to go back and water the plants. When that's done, he cleans up, sweeping away the dead leaves, putting away the tools. His watch says it's just a few minutes before 7 a.m. when he finally lies down, hoping to catch up on a few hours of sleep before Laura arrives.

Yet, try as he might, Antoine just can't fall asleep. Terrified, he feels like he's drowning, watching helplessly as he sinks down into the burning sand of his memories. In anguish, he tosses and turns from one side of the bed to the other. Overwhelmed by this useless agitation, he gets up and paces, back and forth, biting his nails, then lies down again. The hours tick by slowly. One after the other they pass, inexorably, bringing him back to that inescapable moment from his childhood. His thoughts turn again and again to Rosa, who is perhaps sleeping in a room not far from his own.

He ends up falling into a stupor, half asleep, and surrounded, as usual, by grimacing faces. He searches everywhere for Rosa, crossing rivers and streams with a band of ghosts on his heels, waving their arms, moaning, and crying for help. To escape them he has to climb a mountain of corpses, piled up to the sky. Smoke rises violently around him, the odor of charred beams, of sizzling flesh. Beneath his feet, cadavers roll down the mountain, limbs flailing. And Rosa, in a blue and red uniform, her rifle slung on a strap over her shoulder, spits out orders like a dragon spits out fire, and shoots at the cadavers: "Burn the houses! Impale the infants!" Rosa shouts as she takes aim ...

Flames encircle the bed where Antoine sleeps, burning his toes, his feet. They climb up his legs, start licking his torso, climb higher and higher, reach the floor above: Mona's bedroom. That awful crackling that fills his ears, is it the sound of the cradle burning? No! They have to spare the cradle ... Mona's cradle is ... is going to burn ... The white cradle, still intact, engulfed by the flames ... It stands there for a long time, alone, abandoned in the middle of the ruins, and then it disappears ... It has simply ... disappeared. And that heat? Where is it coming from? The fire? Shouldn't it be burned out by now, consumed, extinguished? Shouldn't the pain have been relieved? But the fire isn't dead; it lives in him, because, much to his grief, he is still alive. His ears have heard it all and his eyes have seen it all: the house going up in smoke, walls falling down, grenades exploding, and the atrocious howl of the pack, teeth bared. The murderous pack, behind the sea of hate that hides their faces. Where can he hide? In a bush, a thicket? With the birds? Would they take him under their wings? And the sky, on that April day, the sky ... Nothing but columns of blackish smoke to hold up the vault of the sky, collapsing under the weight of all that hatred. And then the bed falls away, crushed, like the sky, beneath the weight of the cadavers and the hatred. Hatred and blood ... Antoine howls out his dreams, twists and tears at the sheets. He curls up into a ball and moans, because he realizes he is beneath, beneath all those cadavers. He's suffocating. He should wake up, but can't quite come to, because of the circle; the circle, the scent of burning flesh, closes in around him. How many more times will he have to go through this horror before the smell dissipates? The smell of the flesh of his flesh. He is an abandoned scrap of charred flesh. No, he is dissolving, turning into liquid, seeping out at the foot of the bed. He's going to fall, drip away. In just a moment, he will be nothing more than burning tears and, in those tears, he will drown.

As the melancholy toll of a church in the distance chimes noon, Antoine opens his eyes, emerges with relief from that horrible sleep. He notices that while his dreams exhaust him, they no longer terrify him. No, their absence is what would worry him. He picks up a book that he always carries with him and begins to read, wherever his eyes fall on the page: "The monstrous machine couldn't function without the support of many who were complicit, and in the tacit silence of all, the executioners tortured, and the petty criminals helped or watched and sniggered. Alas! From the mechanic working on the convoy that led the deportees to their deaths, to the miserable bureaucrat who updated the files of the victims, there are all too few who are innocent ..."

Is justice, Antoine wonders as he leaves the room to run himself a bath, is justice no more than a mirage? Of all those named as complicit by Jankélévitch, how many were called to answer for their acts? Who, among those who ought to have spoken up, could have broken down the wall of silence and shame to demand that justice be served? How many failed to do so? No, there must exist, there does exist, an ideal of integrity that keeps us from just doing whatever it takes to make peace with our conscience ...

3

Lured in by the call of water, Antoine lets himself slide into the bathtub. His body has become weightless, totally weightless. As have the words and the fury. A wide window looks out on the garden, allowing the bather to imagine he's lying under the trees. The sky is so clear, so calm, so completely neutral. He almost forgets about Rosa, his obsessive quest, and his pain. The water splashes gently. His body relaxes under its caress and he feels himself reborn, back in childhood—no, a time before childhood—a patch of open sky, the sky before a coming storm. There he finds Gala, his grandmother. A large courtyard, a regal breadfruit tree. It's the giant that watches over Gala's kingdom. Gala calls the tree "Monsieur Grand-Bois"—Mister Big Wood. There's a cherry tree, too. It covers the ground with a carpet of red marbles, so full of juice that they look mauve. Crouched at the foot of the tree, Antoine stuffs himself with cherries, shoving them by the fistful into his mouth, just another tender, bloody fruit. He goes into the house, Gala chases him out, calling him *Cochinito*, because he gets everything dirty—the mosaic in the office, the embroidered doilies. For shame—he even leaves fingerprints on Gala's big flouncy skirts.

In the living room stands a kitchen cabinet with glass-paneled doors and shelves lined with bottles—so many mysterious and heavily scented little jars and neatly tied bundles of leaves. Gala insists that each thing have its place. She talks continually, naming everything. Her voice fills the house. When she isn't talking, she's singing. The cabinet, the keys to which are always on her, is called the pantry, or *panetière*. She pronounces it "pané-tierrre" and has forbidden Antoine to touch it. She claims it belonged to her great-great-grandmother. This varnished wooden cupboard holds a special fascination for Antoine. Inside you can find everything you need to make coffee and hot chocolate—bars of chocolate and, of course, sugar. Antoine would trade his greatest treasures to get his hands on Gala's. He's continually eyeing up the bottles, counting them, because, filled with all sorts of fruits and barks, they seem magical. The ones that attract him most are the large, round demijohns. Some are wrapped with a skirt of woven straw. Cherries, peaches, genips, and oranges macerating in an amber-colored liquid that is served only—and he thinks this really unfair—to adults. Gala promises that she'll give him some when he's grown-up. In a little glass with a handle. "But only when you're grown," she repeats each time he begs for a taste. Gala is so exceptionally lucky to possess all those jars filled with brightly colored fruit syrups. He has already thought of getting a stool, clambering up to the *pané-tierrre*, and sipping straight from the jars, but those demijohns are heavy, and the doors are always locked, and the keys—all the keys—are in Gala's pockets. How could he swipe them from her?

Little by little, the liquid in each demijohn takes on the color of the fruits: it grows pink, like unripe cherries, then red. The peach liqueur vacillates between blond, amber, and pink; the orange, a mix of yellow and red, is darker. There is also one that's green, like lime peel. All of these good things are served in those little glasses of which Antoine dreams. Gala calls them her *mamzelles*—little misses. One must, she says, wear long pants to have the right to put your lips on a little miss. That scent of cherries, mixed with the aroma of jams, wild peaches, limes—that's what Gala smells like. It blends with the whiff of boiled sugar, nutmeg, and vanilla that floats in the afternoon air. Peaches and limes come from the mountain, Kenscoff, Furcy. People come down from up there carrying heavy baskets of fruits and vegetables to sell. They all affectionately call Gala "ma chérie" or "ma commère."

Afternoons that ooze tenderness, like delicate white slices of grapefruit that melt in your mouth, slide down your throat. Gala soaks them to remove their bitterness, then, thanks to the magic of sugar and spice, transforms them into delicacies.

Antoine is again swallowed up by another moment, a time of fruits and burned sugar, the time when bees and flies competed with him for the fallen cherries. In the courtyard of the big house, there's a cement basin. The leaves of the breadfruit tree are wide parasols that spread out and dance in the light above the water. Mister Big Wood's leaves, gigantic birds, wrestle furiously with the wind. Other leaves, smaller, wiser, seem to come alive; they shiver, glide gently in the basin's water; sometimes they flit off—little fish that escape, play hide-and-seek. Those leaves come from the pomegranate tree, which lets the wind scatter its white petals across the water.

Antoine is four years old. In the sun, like a star apple, or an overly ripe sapodilla, his skin glistens. He escapes from Gala's arms, dives into the water, swallows a huge mouthful, coughs till tears run down his cheek, and laughs at Gala's panic: "*Ti ason, no!* Little boy, no!" She is afraid he's going to choke. With the help of a towel twisted like a corkscrew, she wants to clean his ears; he hates that and runs off again. She gets angry, but not for long. To calm him down, she improvises a little rhyme, a song she calls *Cochinito, My Little Pig*:

> *Tenia un petite cochon, cochinito, cochinito,*
> *trois fois par jour, on le baignait, cochinito, cochinito,*
> *Mais il avé si peur del agua, cochinito, cochinito,*
> *qu'un beau jour il s'est sauvé, cochinito,*
> *Mon petit cochon, qui me l'a pris?*
> *C'est Grand-Bois, pero, quel bois?*
> *Bois gaïac, que gaïac? Gaïac coq, que coq?*
> *Coq quien chante, quel chante?*
> *Champ de maïs, quel maïs? Cochinito …*

And on she'd go indefinitely, mixing happily, and with a voluptuous pleasure, her two languages. Antoine still remembers the sometimes amused and often critical comments his father made about Gala and her picturesque turns of phrase. Like many folks of his generation, Antoine Guibert, a man of letters, was devoted to the French language and saw any laxness as heading down a slippery slope. According to him, Gala, who'd been living for quite a long time on this side of the island, should have been able to express herself better. But Gala, who had a quick wit, maintained that languages, like songs, could be sung in different keys. I have two countries mixed up in my heart and in my life, two languages that are wedded together like my two islands. They share their winds, their sun, the water of their rivers and streams.

Gala was still singing as she finally caught Antoine. She held him firmly with one hand and, with the other, crushed citronella and orange leaves into the water. That will calm him down, she thinks, because he's a real little demon. The sap runs between her fingers, the water turns greenish. She scrubs his back, belly, head, and legs, leaving red marks on his skin. Be careful, Antoine warns her, don't touch the little pigeon! He'll go pee-pee right in your eyes!

A tender smile brightens Antoine's eyes as he takes this dizzying plunge into his childhood with Gala. Then those verses of Gibran's come flooding back to him:

> *I am dotted silver threads dropped from heaven*
> *By the gods. Nature then takes me, to adorn*
> *Her fields and valleys.*
>
> *I am beautiful pearls, plucked from the*
> *Crown of Ishtar by the daughter of Dawn*
> *To embellish the gardens.*
>
> *When I cry the hills laugh;*
> *When I humble myself the flowers rejoice;*
> *When I bow, all things are elated.*
>
> *The field and the cloud are lovers*
> *And between them I am a messenger of mercy.*
> *I quench the thirst of one;*
> *I cure the ailment of the other.*

In the Dominican Republic, where she was born, Gala had inherited an enormous property, several hectares planted with coffee in Barahona. And when, on that fateful day in 1935, the man named Rafael Leonidas Trujillo ordered the massacre of thousands of Haitian agricultural workers, Gala saved hundreds of lives. In the face of danger and threats, she stood up against the monster. The hyenas paid by Trujillo knew they weren't authorized to invade the hacienda of Gala Limonta de Carvajal, the cursed *"Perejil"*[1] hadn't been able to cross its boundaries.

---

1 The word "perejil" (parsley), in Spanish, is difficult to pronounce for non-native Spanish speakers. In 1937, the Dominican dictator and his men unleashed Operation Perejil, during which Haitians were called to pronounce the fatal word and executed if they failed to do so correctly. It is estimated that 30,000 lost their lives in that massacre.

Suddenly, from the garden, a cry. Antoine shudders, stiffens. He was almost asleep. The water is cold. He shivers, tries to collect himself. He feels so sad, but that doesn't manage to extinguish the exquisite and comforting light that spreads all through him as he remembers Gala. That hooting, so strange: an osprey? Why is it crying? Any small noise puts him on alert.

He slowly emerges from the bath. His feverishness returns; the warm water, the sweet memories only made him feel sluggish. He puts his clothes back on, opens the closet where his things are stored and checks that his suitcase is still firmly locked.

Laura arrives, as agreed, around three in the afternoon. Antoine is ready, a serene look on his face. He's trying to stay calm, keeps repeating that he must. When Laura arrives, he notices the sullen expression in her eyes.

"Hello, Laura!" he calls out enthusiastically. "You look tired."

"Right you are. I didn't sleep much after leaving last night. And no time for a siesta today, either. And you? Were you able to get some rest? Not too homesick?"

"I didn't sleep for very long, but I'm OK. The air here is excellent, invigorating."

"Me," Laura sighs, "if I don't go to bed as soon as I feel tired, usually around midnight, well, then I just have to wait until the next night."

"That's what makes you look so stressed," Antoine says pointedly. "You need to take time to rest … Even if you aren't taking care of your aunt yourself, you have to keep an eye on her. That's an enormous responsibility! I'm sure I'm overstepping here, and I'm sorry about that, but it takes energy to do your job. You have to look out for yourself!"

Antoine stops short, surprised at his own audacity. He expects the young woman to put him in his place, but she says nothing. So, as they quickly head along the walkway toward Rosa's house, he continues:

"If you were to fall sick, I'd have to take care of you. That wouldn't really bother me, but it wouldn't be easy! So, take time to rest."

"You're right. I am tired, but I won't be able to rest until she's gone …"

The gilded doorframe—a poor imitation of rococo style—gives a hint of the jarring décor inside the house. Antoine stifles a grimace of disgust when he lifts his head and discovers, above the lintel, Caryatids of molded plastic, made to look like stone. Still grumbling, Laura turns the key.

"What could be more absurd than this sort of existence? A woman alone, unable to care for herself, walled up in this monumental building that could, I swear, house at least three families ..."

"Have you ever thought of putting her in a nursing home?"

"I've tried everything! Each time, she refuses. I'd have to take her there by force!"

The house smells stale, dusty. Near the entrance, a dog lies on a cushion. He grumbles, but doesn't put too much effort into it. As soon as he senses Laura's presence, he makes a half-hearted effort to wag his limp tail.

"I don't have time to give you a tour," Laura declares, her impatience showing. You'll take a look around if you want to. Upstairs, just like here, you'll find the same series of unused rooms, chockfull of furniture." As she heads up the stairs, she adds, "When you think that she hasn't even left her room for the past two years ..."

Laura gives two loud raps on the door and turns the handle.

"Good afternoon, Aunt Rosa!"

The one who asks to be called Aunt Rosa leans against a pile of cushions and pillows, at the far end of an immense canopy bed. A black scarf is wrapped around her head, but you can still glimpse the strange bald-patch above her forehead. Her swollen face, her globulus eyes—Antoine concludes that it must be from thyroiditis—and her greenish tint recall an amphibian about to explode. Her fingers, swollen with edema, are twisted like talons on the purple velvet quilt. How does she manage to fit so many rings on her fingers? Aghast, Antoine notices a gaudy marquise-cut stone on the index finger of her right hand, a ruby the size of a quail egg.

The bedclothes give off a musty odor, tinged with the slightly sweet smell of camphor and, Antoine senses, uric acid.

"It's the oil she rubs on her hands," Laura explains, visibly ill at ease.

She quickly crosses the room, opens the door to the terrace, and props up the windows, all the while thinking, "How is it possible that I've gotten used to such a disgusting smell?"

"Aunt Rosa, I'm here with the new nurse. His name is Guibert, Antoine Guibert. Aunt Rosa, don't you have something to say?"

Clearly struggling to keep her voice from trembling, Laura adds:

"You could make an effort to be polite, just for once. Everyone is bending over backwards for you!"

Silence.

"Oh well, whatever ..."

Lying deep in the bed, the woman visibly stiffens when she hears the name of the new arrival. A smirk, hard and crass, flitters across her lips, while her eyes, full of dread, shift from Laura to Antoine.

Standing by the door, Antoine seems ready to flee as fast as he can. He feels a wave of heat flood through his body. He's caught in the flames. The acrid smell fills his belly, his throat, rises up to cloud his brain. He tenses all of his muscles and repeats, like a mantra, "Go into that room, stare back at her, do not fall apart like an idiot in front of her, and most of all, most of all, do not start speaking right away." He has always promised himself that he would weigh each of his words before they crossed his lips. Yet, at that moment, he feels the words rising up like a violent tide, a sort of madness, a flow of lava, ready to burst out. They're going to explode, scatter in a myriad of sharp sounds or a cacophony of guttural sounds. He takes a few steps back, closes his eyes for a moment. "You've made it all the way here, just a little more to go!" he tells himself before reopening his eyes and seeking out Laura's. She lays an ice-cold hand on his forearm.

"Are you feeling ill? I've spoken to you twice now and you haven't answered. I thought you were going to faint."

Relieved that he hadn't fallen apart, Antoine stammers, "Excuse me. I just had a dizzy spell."

"It's the camphor! Me too, I just can't take those violent scents. But you also shouldn't underestimate how tiring your trip was. Did you even have lunch?"

Antoine barely manages to answer, and Laura thinks he won't stay long either. He's too delicate to take care of Rosa. She feels the exasperation well up within her. She's going to have to call the agency again, go through all the steps to find and recruit another nurse. But this time she's determined to take the time necessary to find someone who won't immediately run off, even if that means trying a different agency. She'll put an ad in the *Courrier de Nice* or maybe even in a daily paper in Marseille; she'll offer quadruple the going rate. If she has to, she'll pay the cleaning woman to spend the night with Rosa for a while; she'll tempt her with a wad of cash—that's the only language that Marie understands. But I'm done twisting myself into knots for Aunt Rosa! If I owe her a lot—as she always said—I've already repaid her a hundred times over. My debt is paid off!

"OK," Laura begins, breaking the terrible silence that reigns in the room, "Aunt Rosa, now I have to go. Antoine will take care of you. He's Julien's replacement. You know, I told you that already. Me, I have work to do, so I'm off."

Apparently mesmerized by each other, neither Rosa nor Antoine reacts to her words—they just continue to stare. Antoine's reaction—disconcerting to say the least—worries Laura.

"I'm leaving now," she announces again, as if trying to convince herself that it's OK to leave them alone together. "I don't need to wait around any longer, do I, Antoine? You're ready to step in?"

Her voice rises from hesitant to a screech. She's already at the door, ready to flee, but then she turns back and hands Antoine the keys.

"Here, you take them. This key chain is really smart, a sticker on each key tells you what it's for."

She can't get rid of the keys fast enough, as if the key chain had turned into a burning ember.

"Take a tour of the house, if you'd like. Aunt Rosa really gets to me when she refuses to do her part," Laura confides as she leaves the room, in a tone that hints at resignation. "You saw, she didn't say a word!"

"Does she always behave like that?"

"It's her way. She can spend whole weeks like that. Once I thought she'd completely lost the ability to speak. But don't worry about it. She'll end up opening her mouth when she wants to insult you. And that's torture, believe me."

Antoine keeps quiet, leaving Laura to wonder what she could say to reassure him. Since she can't quiet her own concerns, she rushes off down the stairs. Antoine follows her. Suddenly she spins around.

"I almost forgot. I stopped by the bank this morning."

She hands him an envelope that she pulls from her bag. Her hands are trembling.

"There's your salary for the month. I've doubled the amount asked for by the agency. This one—she hands him a second envelope—is for expenses, in case I need to go away for a few days. Just keep track of the receipts, please. Now all I have to do is to wish you good luck!"

She hurries down the last few steps.

"You have my number at the bistro. This one is my home number—she hands him a card. If necessary, call me."

4

With Laura gone, Antoine suddenly feels the urge to rush back to the bedroom and settle accounts with Rosa right away. After all, he tells himself, that's why I've come to this sinister place. He hurries back up the stairs, taking big deep breaths, as if the air around him was growing thin.

"I have no need," he proclaims, "for that vain, noble heart of the crusader for justice. The hour of truth has rung, Rosa Bosquet!" Then he hears himself announce, "I know full well you immediately recognized me as your victim from long ago. We have the same look in our eyes, my father and I, the same height, the same tone of voice."

But right when his foot hits the top step, he sees an image of himself: a hunter who has finally cornered his quarry after a long chase. His head spins and his heart races. Caught up in an emotion as raw as the desire for justice that grabbed hold of him long ago, he fears he will not be able to see this through. His hand clenches the railing; his legs are both leaden and weak. Two days before, everything seemed so clear, but now his glorious confidence has ebbed away.

"I am no hero," Antoine murmurs. "I don't want to be a hero, but what can I do not to become an assassin?"

Slowly, and as if with regret, he walks past Rosa's room, opens the next door and heads out onto the terrace, where he catches a glimpse of Laura, a small dancing spot, hurrying down the road toward the bistro. In the sparkling afternoon light, her pale-yellow cotton skirt with white lace flounces reminds him of butterfly wings. With her thick mane of hair pulled back, her round face looks like that of a child, Antoine muses. How old could she be? Thirty-five—certainly no more ... Laura, Antoine is sure of it, is one of those beings broken all too early by life. To keep from sinking like wrecks to the ocean floor, they grab on tightly, vainly seeking shelter in an empty space, and spend their whole lives hanging, suspended over the abyss, like sausages that never completely dry. Their resigned watchfulness transforms them, within as without, chiseling away till it reaches the stone core of their soul. Their features and their bodies are marked by their evident lethargy, engraved with a sort of agelessness or arrested development, a sullen springtime that leaves them half alive. They live in a desert—no hurry, no hint of regret, but they miss every opportunity. He'd had the chance to consider the generous plumpness of Laura's fingers. Their touch must be soft on the cheek, like Gala's.

The terrace is empty. The furniture must have been removed recently. In one corner, a little glass-topped table. On it, a cup, holding what must be rainwater and a cigarette butt. Here and there, little clumps of earth and faint rusty circles suggest that there used to be potted plants. Did Rosa take care of them herself? he suddenly wonders. Why, at that precise moment, does he think of the plants that used to sit on that terrace, and of Rosa, leaning over them, watering them? Inexplicably unsettled by that image, he lifts his eyes and contemplates the sky and the rocky peaks all around, swathed in the afternoon's pinkish light that embraces everything and encourages us to believe in the innate good of human beings. He questions the trees and the boulders, calls on the swallows circling in the distance. Most of all, he speaks directly to the sky, because he no longer knows if he is at the start or the end of a story. All this beauty so close to Rosa! To Antoine's mind, it's just unfair. He can't foresee the end of this adventure, which he'd hoped for with all of his heart, and for so many years. How many times had he dreamed of meeting Rosa?

He remembers one summer in his hovel in Marseille. Three days and nights, wracked by fever, a fever caused by his stunned realization that he'd stupidly been had, that he'd lost a considerable sum to a con artist posing as a bloodhound. Believing he was on a trail that would inevitably lead him to Rosa, he had met the man in a smoky joint near the port, la Canebière. Without thinking, he'd paid the sum demanded without asking for any guarantee. For several days, he waited for a call from the so-called detective. He sweated and lost his mind, imagining a sort of heart-pounding game, a treasure hunt that would end with him trapping Rosa. He had always promised himself he would lead her along a path of his own choosing, doling out hints to her, one by one, as if from an eyedropper. He had dreamed of giving her the rope with which she'd tie her own halter, of slowly leading out the line, like a lure, tempting her to sink her fangs into it.

With that memory, Antoine feels himself falling into the well of shame and humiliation that is always lying in wait. Then, suddenly, he asks himself just what is stopping him from rushing at that pile of flesh and getting rid of the hag once and for all? "What will killing her get you? The pure and simple satisfaction of eliminating her, like any assassin? Rosa doesn't deserve such a death. Look at your hands: they are beautiful, fine, clean, made to offer caresses, like Gala's, to give life, make it blossom. These hands were given to you so you can love: brotherly hands, a lover's hands, they do not belong to a killer. You need to be careful, Antoine, make sure you don't sully your quest with the brutality of the jackal."

He thinks back to the awful story of Pablo Molina, a Chilean friend, left limping, demolished, forever damaged by Pinochet's prisons. Pablo, whose teeth were all ruthlessly pulled out by dogs of Rosa's ilk. Pablo, torn apart like some cheap toy by bloodthirsty barbarians. Pablo was only seventeen when he fell into DINA's clutches. They'd turned that jovial boy into a tattered rag, a soulless body, exiled from himself. An eternal refugee, Pablo dragged his suffering all around Paris. "*I yam Chilean*," he said, by way of introduction, then quickly lowered his eyes. Pablo's Chile was a dizzying mix of shame and suffering, nostalgia and anger; it was fear and that wild love of one's native land inextricably bound. For all the harm they had inflicted on Pablo, Antoine concludes, Rosa must pay! For all the others, all the torturers around the world, all her acolytes, living or dead, she will pay!

Before returning to Rosa, Antoine decides to look around the house. Armed with the key chain, he leaves the terrace and heads up the stairs. Everywhere, the same lugubrious atmosphere, and that persistent musty smell; he feels like he's going to suffocate. He realizes it's because there's no circulation, but there's also something absolutely unbearable floating in the air, the heavy breath exuded by all those weighty things, the thick curtains that block out the sun. In every room—there are about ten on the upstairs floor—there are piles of mismatched furniture and strange bibelots, peculiar and frightening. Pictures on the walls, reproductions of works by famous painters, a jumble of eras and styles, all hung in an indescribable disorder.

Antoine moves closer to look at the details of a canvas framed in red and gold. He retches and pulls back, a shiver of horror running up his spine. A scene from a bullfight, totally petrifying: a man gored by a bull, abandoned to the animal's fury, while, in the stands, crowds of impassive spectators watch on. Lying on his side, the toreador protects his belly with his arms as the beast attacks his ribs. Both are swimming in a sea of blood. Alongside images of Christ dripping in blood, of Mary and other weeping virgins, there are more scenes of corridas in garish colors. They rub shoulders with Byzantine icons, works by the Haitian painter Préfète Duffaut and Le Douanier, Henri Rousseau, including an enormous reproduction of *Tropical Forest with Monkeys*. An oversized copy of the Mona Lisa is flanked by two enormous canvases inspired by Vodou practices. It's an orgy of loud colors, a real mishmash, Antoine thinks. What really matters to this woman, he realizes, is that she owns it all. She must buy any and everything, wherever she can, like a glutton stuffing her face, as if buying with no sense of taste and without restraint could cure her of some mysterious ailment. He can't contain his exasperation when his eyes fall one last time on the bloody tableau. He grabs a large crystal vase from a marble-topped side table and throws it as hard as he can at an armoire, whose glass doors explode: "Money just burns a hole in their pockets!" His voice echoes strangely with the tinkling of shattering glass and crystal.

He slams the door violently and heads into another room where giant wardrobes overflow with boxes of shoes, expensive clothes, hats, coats. One closet is filled with mink coats, stoles of sable and fox, and so many other furs, all rotting. They say that the female rabble that squirmed in the presidential palace, the entourage of the wives of the Father of the Nation and his son and successor, would fill vast cold rooms with artificial snow and hold sumptuous balls, just to have an excuse to wear their furs of marten, sable, mink, and astrakhan. Antoine promises he'll come back one evening and collect those expensive coats and high-priced gowns to dress Rosa up. "Just to have some fun, I'll throw one last ball for you, you old monkey!" he grumbles.

The immense vestibule is filled by an imposing oak desk, covered with gilt and appliqué. Antoine tries to open each drawer, one after the other—there are at least ten of them—and all resist. In a rage, he tries to force them open. He doesn't fully understand why he has this strange feeling, the impression that this piece of furniture with drawers locked tight is defying him. "Tomorrow," he promises himself, "I'll come back with the tools to open it up. Even if I have to break it to pieces, I'll get it open." He doesn't know, no longer knows what he's really looking for, but he's certain he'll find it there.

Taking an outside stair, he reaches the garden and begins a careful study of the whole property. He realizes that this whole, huge house, which once belonged to some count or lord, was really built long ago. It had been renovated, its façade sanded, other modifications made, some improvements. The ancient doors had clearly been replaced—no doubt because of an unhealthy concern for security—with metal doors: less massive, but painted to look just like wood. Other updates had been purely wasteful, useless tinkering born of megalomania. For example, the arrow slits added along both sides of the building. They must have cost a fortune to put in, given the thickness of the walls, just like the little towers that decorated a sort of walkway around the roof of the east wing. Wrought iron grills had been placed over all the windows, without exception. What a pitiful woman, a pitiful murderer, Antoine repeated, his voice cracking.

Having finished his tour, he has no other choice but to head back to Rosa. Pausing in the doorway, he takes a deep breath, then pushes open the door, steps into the bedroom, and, standing at the foot of the bed, checks his watch: it's 5 p.m.

5

Two of the cushions that had been propping the woman up have slipped and are lying on the parquet. Antoine bends down to pick them up.

"Hououuuuuuuunn! Lauraaaaa!"

The woman emits a dull groan that suggests her fear, but also betrays her defiance. Speechless, Antoine gets up, steps back, and stares at her. With a wild look in his eyes, he stands up tall and sweetens his voice.

"Pray what is the problem? If ..." he begins slowly, "if ... I understand well, you'd like to prevent me from coming too close? But that's just not going to do, Rosa Bosquet. Whether you like it or not," he continues, using the familiar "tu," "I am here to take care of you. I am the new nurse, Laura told you that. You didn't deign to reply when she made the introductions, you didn't unclench your teeth for even one instant, but that's your choice!"

Antoine pulls an armchair toward him. He sets it in front of the bed and lets himself fall into it.

"So, you are Rosa Bosquet ... Me, I'm Antoine Guibert. You know that already, but it's worth repeating! I'm not offering to shake your hand—that doesn't matter to me, and you'd certainly begin bellowing. And then, I give you my word, there's no use crying. I intend to stay here as long as it takes ..."

"Hoooouuuunnnnnn! Lauraaaa!"

"Perched up here on this mountain top, your house is really isolated. You can roar all you like, till you're blue in the face, no one will hear you! I had to fight to get this job, and I'll fight to keep it. It didn't make it any easier for me that the agency was offering double the going rate; an impressive number of candidates were ready to rush over to Gourdaix, a real El Dorado. Nowadays, when everyone's a little short, you just can't imagine how many people looking for work would be willing to go into exile up here for a quarter of that. Between sea and mountain, Gourdaix dominates the coast, an unbeatable view, an amazing location, a lone rocky peak in the heart of the Mediterranean; Gourdaix, the most beautiful postcard from the South of France! You must be dying to know why the agency decided to send me? I had an ace up my sleeve, you know that, right? No? It's simple, really: my talent for writing! Maybe something I inherited from my father?"

"Hooooooouuuuuuunnnnnn ... Hooooouuuuunnnn ... Lauraaaaa ..."

"As you know, Antoine Guibert was one of the best journalists of his day, a caustic and very sharp pen. So, I was chosen for my aptitude for writing, and also my three years of medical school. You insisted that they send you a nurse who was also a good scribe, so here I am!"

"Hooooooouuuuunnnnn! Hooooouuuuunnnn! Lauraaaaaa!"

With his arms crossed, Antoine now paces back and forth as he speaks, his feet echoing loudly with each step. Suddenly, he checks his watch.

"My word," he exclaims, "the time is flying by and you, you just watch me and howl. What are you hoping for, Rosa Bosquet? To hypnotize me, to subdue me? Is this some sort of ritual, an initiation? You decided to hire someone—who happens to be me— to help you to write your memoirs. I swear on all that I hold most sacred, the memory of my near and dear, I swear, I won't be paid just to do nothing. Let's get to work, straightaway!"

In one leap he is at her bedside and grabs what he thinks is a big block of paper. Rosa pulls up the covers around her.

"But ... these are your notebooks?"

From beneath a cushion, Antoine pulls out a pile of notebooks with cardboard covers.

"This is where you are giving birth to your masterpiece! Let's take a look ..."

He holds out his hand.

"Houuuuuuuuuuuuunnnnnnnnnnnnnnnnnnnnn!"

A long, strident cry bursts from Rosa's chest and echoes across the vast, deserted residence. Spontaneously, Antoine pulls back his hand. Then he recoils in feigned surprise.

"Well, well, now ..." he murmurs. "I understand why nurses don't stay long here. Let's be clear about things: You're going to have to adjust to the new rules; otherwise, I'll gag you and then gather up all this nonsense"—he points at the notebooks—"and burn it!"

Ignoring his patient's grimaces and grunts, Antoine tugs on the covers, tosses cushions all over the room, then grabs the pile of notebooks and places them right next to the door so he can take them away later.

"You know full well, Rosa, that my presence here is not a question of chance. Let's say that chance came to my rescue, that sometime chance works in mysterious ways, it's true. Remember that old proverb: 'One day for the hunter, one day for the prey.' Today, someone else is wearing the boots and holding the crop, Rosa Bosquet. His name is Antoine Guibert. You heard that, right? Gui-bert ... Antoine Guibert!" he shouts, articulating each syllable with care.

His body shuddering spasmodically, he moves back toward the bed.

"From now on, I am the master here, Rosa. I will crush you under my boots like a flea, a roach, an earthworm. I'll flatten you, no mercy!"

He pretends to squash something under his heel, producing a terrible grinding noise; Rosa shudders, as if having a seizure.

"Maaa ..."

"There's no one to hear your bellowing, Rosa," Antoine spits out, his voice hard. "There's just the two of us—you and me. You and me in this immense house! What did you think? That you were one of the chosen, that you'd never be called to account? That you'd be able to sleep without a care, snuggled warmly in your bed? That you'd enjoy the peaceful sleep of the innocent until the end, and die at a ripe old age? Nothing to say, Rosa? Surprising. Then I'll just keep on talking, and you will listen. I'll talk until we both croak. For as long as I have words with which to whip you, you'll listen to me! You'll listen to my voice until it dies, wiped out. Word by word, you'll learn of my despair; you'll retrace with me, step by step, the paths of my distress. It was hard work to find you. I put my whole life on hold to look for you, and gave up everything for this one moment when I would finally stand before you. Wavering between hope and despair, like a madman searching for gold, I looked for you. Impelled by an unshakable faith and by my conviction—which never left me—that justice must be served."

With her head bowed, Rosa observes her adversary from beneath her lowered lids. Her chin is pulled back into her neck. Under the covers, her chest rises and falls with the rhythm of her breathing; then, slowly, she sits up and, with a calculated intensity, fixes her cold dry eyes on Antoine, intensely examining his face. Without a word, they size each other up, and Antoine knows for certain that not only will Rosa never feel repentance, she is of another species. He runs through all the most terrifying animals; none of them can hold a candle to his adversary. They say that alligators are without pity; she must be of the same species as they: a ferocious reptile, venomous and cruel, as only those animals can be. He feels it in the hostility of her gaze. All that follows will stem from this first jousting match. Whatever the cost, he must win this first round, impose his will on the beast—whatever the cost. She must understand that, from then on, he will be the master. How long does this contest of wills last? Antoine has no idea. Just as he leaves the room, he notices, at the foot of the bed, the old mangy dog, with droopy ears and dull eyes, sheepishly observing him in silence. Coming close to the animal, he declares:

"You, too, are just a dirty beast. You'll only make the sheets even dirtier. Come here!"

He grabs the animal by the scruff of its neck and tosses it in the dog bed by the door, while Rosa thrashes and starts howling again. With his foot, he pushes the dog bed out of the room.

"Tomorrow I'll take it to the pound," he announces.

Merciless, he reiterates his order that Rosa be quiet, immediately. Otherwise, he'll make the dog suffer the same fate she had imposed on Mélanie's dog.

At those words, Rosa wavers, then begins wailing again. Antoine comes back and leans down over the bed. He comes very close to her, cups his hands together and then seizes her by the neck and huffs, huffs and howls, as loud as he can.

"You miserable woman! You want to damn me, that's right. You want to complete your life's work, but I won't give you the chance! I am here to make you pay for all your wicked murders, even that of Mélanie's poor puppy, stomped under your heel! Do you remember, Rosa? Tell me, do you remember Mélanie Brénus? There you go, howl some more, let's talk about Mélanie's dog! That macabre story must absolutely figure in your memoirs, because writing your memoirs means promising to tell the truth, the whole truth, nothing but the truth! A courageous undertaking—bold,

Marie-Célie Agnant

even, to the extent that you have to resist the temptation to conceal certain unappetizing facts. On that day, not satisfied with having killed the animal by stomping it under your foot, you aimed your pistol at Mélanie and forced her to cook up a purée of dog and eat it while you watched. Do I have to tell you that Mélanie never got over it? She spent the rest of her life in an asylum, howling from evening till daybreak, just like a dog howls at death.

"Hoooooouuuunnnn!"

"What's this!" Antoine exclaims, finding something under the bed.

He bends down and picks up a notebook, then reads the thick block letters on its cover: *Memoirs of Rosa Bosquet.*

"Well, well! This one must have slipped out when I grabbed the others. How presumptuous you are!"

Antoine shakes his head in disbelief.

"You want to write your memoirs? A fantasy born of senility? Narcissistic neurosis? It's so hard to believe! Is it a book of unbelievable stories? Of marvelous tales? A saccharine novel? A detective story? Is it a book aimed at a small group of false friends, faithful allies, or flatterers? A book for real readers or idiots? According to the agency, it's supposed to be your memoirs. The dictionary defines that genre as follows: 'A written record that a person makes of events in which they took part or which they witnessed.' In some sense, then, they're confessions. Considering the role you played all those years, your confessions will certainly be connected to historical events that you can't dress up! Will there be a foreword? You must have something in mind, unless it's already written; I imagine it stuffed with trite expressions and outdated clichés, like 'in order that no one ignore ...,' or even, 'for the edification of all.' Well no! You'll have to replace all those hypocritical and awkward turns of phrase with real sentences ... So, let's get to work, shall we?"

He stands at attention.

"General Bosquet! I will not leave this room. Your ghost writer, at your service!"

Antoine settles himself comfortably in the armchair at the foot of the bed and opens the notebook.

"But ... it's a blank notebook! Is it the one you were getting ready to start? Very well. We'll get down to work right away. 'In the month of April, 1964, I, Rosa Bosquet, killed with my own hands the journalist Antoine Guibert, father of the man now sitting before me; then I set fire to his home and caused the deaths of all the other members of his family!'"

"Houuuuuunnnnnnnnnnn! Houuuunnnnnnn!"

As Antoine begins to write furiously, the woman's eyes are filled with fury. She growls, letting loose with a trumpet blare even louder and longer than the previous ones.

"Don't growl; it's no use. If you really want to write your memoirs, you just can't omit that episode."

Antoine unbuttons his shirt; he's suddenly very hot, sweating profusely.

"What you are going to write, what we will write together, Rosa, is a book about your career as a torturer and assassin. You're so smart, you knew that the moment I set foot in this room. You understood right away that I wasn't here to earn my pittance, nor for the pleasure of wiping your old monkey ass. No, I repeat, I am Antoine Guibert ... son of Antoine Guibert, a journalist for the daily *La Patrie*, who, forty years ago, met his death thanks to the murderous bullets from your pistol. So, this is what we write: "I, Rosa Bosquet, killed with my own hands the journalist Antoine Guibert and all of his family along with him!"

"Houuuuuuuunnnnnn! Houuuuuuuunnnnnnnn!"

The bald Gorgon roars, her eyes shot through with red, a mix of fear and hatred. Not knowing how to stem the tide of her fury, Antoine folds himself in, as if he were cold. Pulling his neck down into his shoulders, he whistles through his teeth.

"Forty years I've been waiting to catch you!"

Suddenly, he begins to pace like a wild beast, circling the bed and moaning all the while.

"Antoine disappeared, then Antoine came back, Rosa, forty years later! Antoine Guibert, right here in front of you, in flesh and blood, in your lair. And he's the one who's going to give birth to your masterpiece! I could create a truly marvelous autobiography for you, you know? To make it really authentic, I'll dig into the documents I brought with me. I've carted along a whole suitcase full of papers and photos. You'll be thrilled to see them, to see yourself in action again. In one of them, certainly the most eloquent, you're wearing a white blouse. A memorable snapshot! There you are, with your bulging belly, as pregnant as can be, a smoking gun in your right hand. And your white blouse, your pure white lab coat, is stained like a butcher's apron, smeared with fresh blood. Rosa the Butcher! Is it true, Rosa, that your child, the one you were carrying then, didn't survive your crimes? He was born, they say, with his umbilical cord wrapped around his neck. No doubt he committed suicide not to have you as a mother. But you were so elegant when you posed, with your kepi perched on your duck-tail hairdo! It seems that's what they call that work of art you are wearing in a number of those photos. I also found audio tapes, speeches that you gave or wrote for your master, the Unworthy Father of the Nation; transcripts of interviews, but also testimonials about your life, your exceptional career as ..."

Antoine pauses for a moment.

"How should I put it? If you'd been a soldier, one would have simply spoken of your military career. But you weren't part of the army, you were part of the death squads, those famous National Security Volunteers. You were the head of the paramilitary, a *Fillette Lalo*! For you and the others of your band, killing was an instinct. You were a jackal, a hyena, an alligator, all of those beasts at once! Although ... it is unjust to compare you to those beasts, who only attack when they are threatened or starving."

"Hoooooouuuuunnnnnn! Lauraaaaa!"

"A literal translation of that bit of animal speak: Get out of here! Answer: Howl as much as you like, Rosa. I'm going to stay here with you in this awful abode; nothing and no one will make me leave. You'll never get me to leave this room. In fact, I'm going to set up my bed right here in front of yours. I'll put it on a platform, high enough that I can easily see you. And you can be sure that you're the one who'll leave here first—or maybe we'll both leave here together, you in your coffin and me walking behind. So, roar as much as you like, shout up and down the path, it's all the same to me."

Like a burst balloon, Rosa shrivels up. Antoine grits his teeth, howls and storms:

"Yes, I did say 'path'! It's imperative to use the precise term when you're writing, because we are embarking upon a voyage, you and me, Rosa Bosquet; a voyage to the land of hyenas and jackals, assassins and imbibers of blood; a voyage to the land of my suffering. You will need to travel with me down all the paths of distress, Rosa. Tell yourself that you are just a beast, an evil-doing animal that I'm leading by the halter to slaughter!"

Antoine paces frenetically under Rosa's angry glare. Drowning in his own delirium, he doesn't even glance at her anymore, but keeps on ranting just the same. The words flow, like yarn off a spindle, a painful knot buried deep in his gut; a dizzying flow of words, an avalanche of words dangling from the red thread of blood and hatred that stretches between Rosa and him.

"Hoooooouuuuunnnnn! Lauraaaaa!"

Under the mauve comforter, the gelatinous mass trembles.

"You're afraid you've reached your final hour? It's true, there is nothing more cowardly, more of a chicken than a torturer! But remember this: I did not come here to take your life. You won't turn me into a murderer, Rosa Bosquet, even if it would be much simpler to put a period at the end of this story by lodging a bullet—bam!—in your plucked head ... or by suffocating you. What do you think? I could ..."

In one bound he is at the head of the bed and grabs a pillow. He pulls on it so hard that Rosa topples over.

"Note, what I say: I could take this and bring it down over your big fat toad face and press, harder and harder, until you expired. Yet ..." He pauses, still holding the pillow in his outstretched arms, "yet ... my suffering would still be unchanged! But I'd be doing you a great service, because I'm sure that the impunity you've always enjoyed must have ended up feeling like a burden! It surely weighs on you, right? You must have had your fill of impunity, Rosa Bosquet! Now that I really think about it, I won't lift a hand against you. The act of suppressing, destroying the executioner, does nothing to calm or cure the victim. To take your life, I'd actually have to hate you, Rosa, but, frankly, I don't feel any hatred for you. What I feel, believe me, is much stronger and has no name."

He again points an accusing finger at her.

"If I kill you, right now—bam! I'll never know why you did it, what motivated you to do such dirty work, and that is more than I can bear. So, really, as much as you are afraid that I'm going to kill you, I fear that you will die."

Antoine's voice is transformed into a moan as raw emotion and anger put a knot in his throat.

"Rosa Bosquet, today I am a boy, just ten years old, who demands that you explain why all those he loved had to die, are all dead and gone, all ... assassinated by you! You have no idea how determined children can be when they really want to understand something. Today, I am that child who, when just ten years old, witnessed one of your many crimes. And he wants to know just how it is that you never felt any remorse? How is it that your conscience hasn't buckled under the weight of so many deaths? That you never thought of doing away with yourself? In all these years ... forty years. Forty years of emptiness and distress, madness ... All these years, you could have asked for forgiveness a thousand times."

6

Antoine leaves the room, the pile of notebooks under his arm, and heads to the kitchen. He wastes a ton of time searching it from top to bottom, as if expecting to find some hidden secret, before trying to come up with something for Rosa's meal.

Drawers and cupboards are stuffed full of an unimaginable quantity of utensils, pots, and other odds and ends uselessly taking up space. The freezer is overfilled with food: soups, ratatouille, stews, and other dishes, no doubt prepared by Laura. He thinks he recognizes her small, careful script, just like on the envelopes filled with money.

The kitchen is large, filled with light. The oval-shaped table is covered with a cloth in the bright colors of the south of France. Yellow and green ceramic tiles rise up to the ceiling, while pale yellow curtains that billow in the gentle breeze like frilly skirts give the room a bright and welcoming air. In one corner, a wicker birdcage and an aquarium, both empty, bear silent witness to Rosa's isolation. Adjoining the kitchen is an imposing dining room filled with a jumble of cabinets and sideboards, dressers crammed with vases, tea and coffee sets, porcelain, fine crystal, and silver. And beneath a crystal chandelier that might, in its better days, have hung from the ceiling of a cathedral, a table that could easily seat forty guests.

Dinner is simmering. Antoine continues his inspection. In the empty house, his footsteps echo strangely. A vibrating drumbeat that fills the space, a terrifying sound that resonates through his whole body ... Then suddenly, with his hands outstretched, he is propelled toward the sink. Unable to contain his hands' furious rush, he counts: twenty-three ... twenty-four ... Twenty-four knives waiting for him, shiny and new, displayed in a case of the finest wood, there on the wall like books on a library shelf. He can't tear his eyes away from that arsenal; it calls to him, pulling him forward like an animal on a leash. Twenty-four knives: with gleaming handles and steel blades, these knives, like everything else in this house, have never been used. They are there because any kitchen worth the name must display all the tools of the trade. Just one would do the trick ... Antoine compares them, weighs them. "All of them!" he declares, his voice booming in the empty kitchen. One after the other! Let's start with this one, the smallest, the knife with this little hooked tip that I'll slide along from her neck to her bellybutton ..."

His mind spinning out of control, Antoine considers each item in this arsenal assembled just for him. His breath is a deep wheezing, a menacing tide rising to fill the room. His face, dripping with sweat, hangs in pain over the sink. Bent in two, he cries out loudly, imploring that god who has watched over his madness for so many years, but who seems now to have abandoned him. Serrated knife, boning knife, carving knife, long knives, silent and deadly, cleaver, stiletto, cutlass. He names each of them aloud. Old friends long out of sight, he recognizes them. During those years when he was adrift in Paris, he'd been a dishwasher, server, cook's apprentice. He feels strangely happy to have found them here—like true friends, they know the scope of his dreams, the immensity of his despair. In a slow prayer, he recites the verbs, aligning them with the rhythm of his breath: cut, slice, gut, chop, carve, guillotine, section ... He lets water from the tap flow down over his head for a long time. Slowly, slowly it douses the fire within him. His shirt is soaking wet, but so what. He must at all costs drown out those terrifying images—that body withering under the assault of the blades, collapsing with a dull thud, and all that blood ... The blood of the beast, spattered up to the ceiling, covering it; blood that, as soon as it spurts out, grows thick like tar and drips down the walls, oozing puddles that swallow everything up ... Hunt down the animal that is tracking through my guts, Antoine repeats ... Kill the hyena seeking to be born in me, squash the beast before it sees the light of day, he prays, through the stream of water pouring over his face. He towels off his face with his shirt, pats his eyes. He's not sure if he actually cried.

After a while, feeling calmer, he prepares a tray for Rosa. He ladles some leek soup into a bowl, with crackers, ham, and cheese to go along with it. He adds a salad and some fruit compote. The smell of the food is nauseating.

Antoine looks on as Rosa dives into the meal with a fevered gluttony. His stomach heaves as he listens to her slurp it down loudly, one spoonful after the other. She sucks it in avidly, a horrifying concert as the spoon clanks each time against her dentures. She grabs handfuls of salad and shoves them into her mouth, then pops in the crackers. Crumbs are everywhere, dangling from the tuft of hairs on her chin. She seizes the ham and cheese at once, swallows it up and then, in two slurps, downs the compote.

Antoine wonders if she hasn't gone mad. Never in his life has he witnessed such a revolting spectacle. He hurries into the bathroom, coming back with wipes and washcloths, a basin and an ewer of water. He begins to wash her up, surprised that she doesn't complain. Not a word, not a shout, she just lets him do it. He hands her a washcloth that she catches in her gnarled fingers, like a bird of prey snatching a shred of flesh. She awkwardly sponges off her face, then lets him undress her. Antoine changes her dirty nightshirt, horrified by the bedsores that cover Rosa's body. But isn't she just rotten through, inside and out? He tells himself he'll need to get some gloves. Then, ever so carefully, he slips a clean nightshirt on her, taking every precaution to avoid touching that necrotic skin.

"It disgusts me to see you stuff yourself like that! If you could get out of your bed, you'd eat me up in just one big bite. Did you get it into your head that this was your last meal? Are you afraid I'm going to deprive you of food? Answer me, Rosa Bosquet! Just what are you afraid of?"

He leans down over Rosa, who is trembling convulsively, and shouts, like one possessed:

"Answer me! What are you afraid of?"

Rosa recoils as his breath, a wave of fury, spreads over her face.

"Answer, you wretch! Answer me!"

He raises a menacing fist.

"Houuuuuuunnnn! Lauraaaaa!"

Antoine lets his arm fall.

"It's true, you've decided not to speak!"

"So close to the goal, pull yourself together," he orders himself. He steps back and lets himself fall into the armchair. Will he get out of there? Leave Rosa alone for the night?

Then he rises and moves toward her again. She tenses up as hard as she can and begins shouting once more before realizing that he just wants to straighten her bed. Rolling her first to one side and then the other, he smooths the sheets and blankets, wipes away the cracker crumbs, mechanically plumps the pillows.

"I'm out of steam," Antoine announces, "I have to go lie down."

He staggers back toward the villa. "Holy Mother, Holy Mother, I pray to you, come to my rescue," he murmurs. "Tell me ... tell me where to store my anger?" Halfway there, he stops suddenly. He turns around hesitantly and then rushes back to Rosa. Waving his arms, he rants, "That's exactly what I need, right now ... that and nothing but that, right away." A tremor runs through his body; he clenches his teeth and his fists, tight enough to crack them. He hears his blood and the galloping of his heart. His temples are caught in a vise. "Knock her out with the armchair, flatten her, turn her into a pancake of flesh and blood, strangle her. I want to feel ... feel my fists clenched around her neck until she gives her last breath ..."

He turns the handle and the door squeaks open. Eyes bulging in terror, Rosa sits up and opens her mouth. On the bedside table, her dentures float in murky liquid: "Merciful God," Antoine sighs. He gently closes the door and leaves the house, unaware of where he's headed.

Rosa keeps her eyes riveted on the armchair where Antoine had sat all evening, the chair that stands like a jailer at the foot of the bed. She stares at it, as she had earlier stared at Antoine, trying to gather up what remains of her resources to confront her adversary.

Antoine finally makes it back to his room, throws himself down on the bed and immediately falls asleep—like a rock. His sleep is troubled, as usual, wracked by nightmares. He runs in circles around Rosa's house, grabbing objects here and there, tossing them all together in a big pile on the terrace. Wielding an ax, he splits the pieces of furniture: Ungh! Crack! Crack! Ungh! Chairs, tables, and dressers shudder and fall to pieces under the attack: Ungh! Crack! Ungh! Crack! Ungh! A big pile of wood. He builds an immense pyre on top of which reigns the mahogany armchair. Like a man possessed, he rushes around the terrace, splashing it with gasoline. There in the armchair, in the middle of the blaze, is Rosa, her mauve blanket spread out around her. Despite the fire licking her face and the flames swallowing up the blanket, Rosa still smirks and wheezes, "Houuuun … houuuunnnnn!"

At around ten o'clock, the telephone by the front door rings. Jumping awake, Antoine has no idea where he is, no idea where the ringing is coming from. He rubs his eyes and, still haggard, pulls himself together: Rosa! he bellows.

He is in the hills above Gourdaix, at Rosa's. He pales, jumps out of the bed, still tangled in the sheets. His heart, pounding wildly, aches. Then he hears his own voice: "You finally found her. It's really her, Rosa Bosquet. Now you either rise to the occasion, take charge of the situation, or get off stage!"

A few minutes pass. He's aware that his whole life, his very existence, hangs in the balance. The telephone rings again. He hurries over, picks it up, and hears Laura on the other end of the line, in a complete panic. She stammers out a confused and rambling apology, but he doesn't understand what she's going on about and has to ask her to repeat herself. Once he's recovered from his shock, he tries to calm her down, willing his voice to sound reassuring.

"I'll head over there as soon as Marie leaves. Don't worry, Laura."

Antoine had planned to spend a good part of the day exploring Gourdaix. He would have taken the old mule track, the Paradise Trail, all the way to the village of Bar-sur-Loup, then wandered along the narrow streets, meandered through the shops and art galleries. But now Laura is asking him to step in and take the place of the day nurse, who just quit. It bothers him, he realizes, as he slides back into bed. "I don't like it, but how can I say no? Laura has a lot more to complain about than I do!" He admits that he has to salute her determination to juggle and pretend. He remembers her brusque gestures, her clenched lips; all of that fury inside and her efforts to appear indifferent, to silence her pain, while even today, Rosa is still grinding her down! He shakes his head from side to side, a habit of his when he needs to think things through. To lift his spirits, he reminds himself that every cloud has a silver lining, he just has to figure out how to make the best of the situation. The more time I spend with Rosa, the better it will be.

Bolstered by that new conviction, Antoine forces himself to eat a little breakfast—he has at least two good hours before he needs to join Rosa. He goes out for a walk, taking books and a notebook with him. Once outside, he revels in the day. Although it's already late, droplets of dew still glisten on the lawn and on the olive trees' silvery leaves. Under a clear blue sky splotched with lavender, the sun gently grows warmer. The shimmering light filters between the tree branches; birds dart through the rays, tussling and chirping.

He walks, savoring each caress of light on his face. On a marsh, ducklings glide by, quacking. Even today, the sight of birds makes him think of his father, of his fascination with game birds. He clambers up on a stone wall, certainly what remains of some abandoned farm, and watches the flock of wild ducks. Trailing noisily one after the other, they seem to feel an irresistible pleasure as they cut through the smooth surface of the water, leaving a wake of glistening waves behind them. They head into a narrow canal bordered with gorse and a strange variety of lily, pink with dashes of purple, maybe a Martagon lily or Turk's cap. He envies the birds' calmness, their profound nonchalance.

Each day Antoine jots down the steps of his quest in a notebook. That morning, he writes just one sentence, again and again, all down the page: "Justice will be served, justice will reign." Those solemn words, echoes of a far-off time—he must owe them to Gala. But when? What was happening when he heard them? They'd flown so effortlessly from his pen, beside a drawing he'd sketched of a monstrous mollusk with shadowy, bulging eyes.

The two hours of rest pass quickly. When he arrives at Rosa's, just as he starts down the walkway, he comes face to face with Marie, on her way back from the laundry, carrying an armload of freshly washed sheets. She tries to look surprised and, as if to protect herself from some sort of danger, awkwardly clutches the pile of sheets to her. Antoine immediately notices her round cheeks, her ink-black hair that highlights the milky pallor of her skin, but he is especially aware of the curiosity in her eyes, her inquisitive gaze. With a small nod, she moves on ahead. Antoine follows her, noting that her calves are too thick and catching a glimpse, beneath her apron, of her plump, round knees. It brings to mind a cow heavy with a calf and still pulling a cart. That childish idea brings a mischievous smile to his face. "I didn't expect her to be so young, she's not half bad. I'd like to squeeze that plump body of hers, juicy like a good steak, moist and ready to go, but … She seems like she's found her place at Rosa's." He has an inkling that he's going to need to watch out for Marie, with that fake friendly smile of hers, and those glazed eyes—no magic in them at all.

7

Once in the house, he's happy to see that Marie has put more heart into her cleaning—a fresh scent of cleanser and lemon perfumes the air. At the foot of the stairs, he pauses to watch the dust motes floating in rays of sunlight, and in their dance, another page from his childhood slowly unfolds. The light winds and gusts of that season—the only one captured in his memory—leave him shaken. He sees himself as a little boy, on a banister like this one, of cedar or mahogany. In his hands, a rope that he tosses, like a lasso. He scoots along, shrieking happily. He is eight years old, the railing is his horse, he's named it *caballo*. He pronounces it "cabayo," shouts as loudly as he can, much to the chagrin of his mother, who just can't stand such noise. Much later, he learned that he'd called his mount that because of Gala, of her speech adorned with words borrowed from the language she brought back from the other side of the border. Back then, he didn't yet understand the origin of those strange-sounding words, the exquisite and exalting music where r's danced and twirled: *Tonino, me amorrrr, corrrazon, corrrazoncito, a caballo vamos, pero est tiempo de mannger.* Gala might as well have spoken to him in Chinese, Swahili, or Urdu, it would've had the same effect, the same magic, the same joy of sounds from his childhood. How old would Gala be today? Even that, he has no idea. Gala was ageless, she was his grandmother, just Gala.

All of that is lost in the fog, blackish smoke that rises and is carried away by the wind. Nothing remains, nothing will ever remain, but the confusion and pain—insatiable and cruel—that nip at him relentlessly. They say you have to learn to heal, to move beyond the pain. Antoine doesn't believe it. There are ailments from which one never recovers.

He climbs the stairs. On the landing, he freezes. An angry voice giving orders, glacial and perfectly clear.

"I don't want him here! Do you hear me? You have to get rid of that person immediately, I don't want to see him again! Do you understand? Never again! Lying here in my bed—you have no idea just what I'm capable of!"

He waits a few minutes, hears the click of the phone disconnecting. He knocks on the door. Rosa doesn't answer. He knocks louder, still nothing. He turns the handle, steps into the room, and tries to keep his face from betraying his shock.

Marie has tidied up the room, but for some strange reason, she neglected to move the armchair back to its place. It's still right there, facing the bed, where Antoine left it the night before. He sits down, fixes his eyes on Rosa's. His voice dripping with sarcasm, he snaps:

Congratulations! You've found your voice again, all your words, and now you're taking action."

He raises his voice.

"Poor Laura. How can you feel no remorse for abusing her all these years? Poor Laura," he continues, his voice suddenly overcome with exhaustion, "she doesn't know, or doesn't want to know just what you're capable of, but me, I know it all. I know more than you think and you can just forget about making me leave, because I won't. And since writing that book is what's most important, let's just start at the beginning! I know the circumstances that led to your joining the brigade, Rosa Bosquet. So, we're going to tell the whole story, right down to the smallest detail, from your rise through the ranks to your coronation as queen of the *Fillettes Lalo*. In fact, you can just listen, because I've already written all of that for you: Rosa Bosquet wasn't yet thirty years old when she began her career as a torturer in the Casernes Dessalines and at Fort-Dimanche. To understand her path to the top, let's go back to the end of the 1950s. A small town with a most enchanting name: Sialaberim. There, a young woman named Rosa is unable to control her mounting desire for a future. They say she's beautiful, intelligent, but she's almost twenty-five, and she doesn't understand why her life should be nothing but a long, endless wait. All around her, puppets and dolls are busy doing whatever it takes to survive, sleeping with the boot-wearing beasts. Birds of prey, too—lots of those. Rosa refuses to be a puppet, and she doesn't like dolls; she feels a kinship with the birds of prey. When she watches them circling high above, her heart begins to pound as if she were regaining a long-lost memory. She has no idea what will come to release her from her waiting, but she hopes for it; not for a miracle, that's just something for old women with empty, sagging breasts, who spend their days in churches, praying with their arms outstretched, surrounded by the stale odor of candles and their own faded skirts. No, she wants to be a woman who displays her breasts proudly, covered in jewels and the best perfumes. She wants to have it all—and nothing less. So she hopes, with all her heart, calls out for an act of magical alchemy that will bring together the puppet, the doll, and the bird of prey, and give birth to the most fearsome predator that has ever existed: the *Fillette Lalo*.

In 1960, Haiti burns with a fever that no water from any river could ever calm. Those who are drawn to the corridors of power seem motivated by a new-found energy that intoxicates them, pushes them to commit the most barbaric acts in hopes of getting into the good graces of the new president, a small, most unremarkable man, who came into the palace like a jack-in-the-box, the sort of surprise tailor-made for banana republics. Both feared and despised, that pitiful grey doctor—Papa Doc, as he's sometimes called—has a shocking ability to control others, and he uses it on everyone. That's how so many influential businessmen, esteemed doctors, lawyers and other professionals, respected family men, and even men of the cloth, will leave their positions to jostle others at the doors of the presidential palace, to put on a uniform made of rough blue cloth and serve the tyrant. The Father of the Nation promises to transform all of his new recruits into figures both feared and revered. The trials are demanding, the paths leading to the upper echelons riddled with traps. But what does that matter? One brother will give up his sister in order to wear the uniform and have his share of power, a husband will sell his wife to the highest bidder. And yet a third, who was refused the honor of wearing the blue uniform, will still volunteer to join a midnight raid to capture his own brother-in-law, accused of being part of a plot to blow up the presidential palace. Afterwards, he'll appear before the tyrant, dressed in a blood-red shirt to deliver a trophy in an ice-bucket: the head of the rebel brother-in-law.

What are all these accursed words that explode, willfully transgressing all limits and borders? A curse upon those who take on the difficult and perilous task of trying to understand! Those who dare to ask questions pay dearly for it. It's in that toxic environment that the young Rosa decides to develop a plan of attack, to put an end to her maddening wait. She's a bird of prey and it's past time for her to build her own nest. She moves in with a young lawyer who has just joined the Father of the Nation's service, filling the highly desired role of political advisor and ghost writer with exceptional efficiency, drafting the speeches the despot uses to spread terror. His office, on the ground floor of his home, is not far from the presidential palace and the barracks where the gang in blue parades and preens. Very quickly, a cohort of young officers who dream, just like him, of rapidly climbing to the top, start coming to him for advice. And very quickly, too, his young wife starts offering her own advice to all those uniformed gentlemen, their asses perfectly molded in khaki trousers. Like so many other women, Rosa is crazy for that uniform, symbol of unlimited power, but most of all, she is attracted by the weapons those men carry, those revolvers that add weight to their steps and that they adjust every now and again, with a gesture meant to be both elegant and provocative.

The overly ambitious little lawyer doesn't worry at all about who his wife spends her time with; he has other cats to skin. He has no need for women, especially now that he's comfortably ensconced in his position. Men also try to woo him. If he only had more time, he'd take full advantage of that manna. Everything is working just fine. He has the ear of the Father of the Nation. In the street, people bow and step aside so he can pass, and everyone praises his wife to the heavens.

In compensation for the services she provides the dashing officers, the young woman—then known only as Rosa—asks for just one thing. With trembling mouth and hands, her eyes riveted on the desired object, she begs to play with their pistols! Dumbstruck, those novices quickly take off their gun belt and offer her their weapon. Her face ecstatic, transformed by a silent wave of pleasure, Rosa takes hold of the object, caresses it, and babbling incomprehensible sounds that frighten several among them, pretends to take aim at those she calls her little soldiers. She rubs the weapon across her cheeks, on her lips, her sex; her entire body begins to shudder and shake. And that's when—only then— she takes them into her, wrapping them in a bitter embrace, both savage and short-lived. She seems to want to suck them down, to swallow them whole to fill some dark chasm within her. But once they leave, she feels even emptier than before, wracked by a hunger far more intense and insatiable that eats away at her, because she knows that out in the hallways, those young bastards make fun of her, despise her, snigger together as they compare their exploits.

And then one day, she finds in her husband's office a plan for the formation of a special brigade. On the order of the Spiritual Leader, the lawyer wrote up a communiqué to be printed on the front page of all the newspapers. Addressed to the men and especially the women of good will, it exhorts them to sign up to defend the country against the threat of an invasion by expatriates who want to strip the sons of the nation from power and replace them with a criminal socialist system, imported from a neighboring island. "Grenadiers Attack!" reads the headline. The Father of the Nation is counting on women to sign up, on "those who give life to be equally able to protect it." In a flash of illumination, our Rosa hears her calling, her salvation. She is among the first to appear at the recruiting office on the Champ de Mars, to put on the blue uniform and have the red kerchief knotted around her neck by the nasal-voiced midget. Rosa returns home that day, with a kepi on her head and a pistol on her hip, and she shuts her door to the little officers who gossip and sneer, promising herself that she'll make them swallow their words, that she'll reduce them to nothing.

Rosa's first act is to draw up a list of all the officers who taught her to aim and handle a pistol, those that she welcomed into her bed, that she straddled while holding their weapon to their temple. She makes the Father of the Nation believe that they—there were nineteen of them—are plotting to assassinate him. One night, the Father of the Nation gathers them all together. Rosa and her band of acolytes, Juste Bertrand, Franco Nero, and Daisir, lead the operation. The officers she accused are taken to a field outside the city, on the Cul-de-Sac plain, where an open pit had been dug. Over the following weeks, the voice of the Supreme Leader reads the roll-call on the radio. To terrify the people, he calls each name and answers for them: "Absent!" A few days after this bloody purge, the Supreme Leader names Rosa the *Reine-Choche*—the Devil Queen—and entrusts her with the command of the National Security Volunteers.

"Tell me, Rosa, are you happy with this beginning? You see, I didn't miss a single word from the mouths of any of the informants I found in New York, Miami, Montreal. I must say it's your fault I ended up spending time in nasty dives with unrepentant big mouths, shriveled up by their own impotence and cowardice. They enjoy telling anyone who'll listen everything they've picked up here and there about the infernal dictatorship. I was dumbfounded when I realized the most atrocious acts committed by members of your clique had become just random anecdotes. In a café in Montreal, I saw a man—his eyes shining, clearly enjoying the moment— recount Mona's murder. He didn't know he was talking about my sister. Had he known, I don't think it would have slowed him down at all. He gave an impassioned description of the events of April 1964, as if he'd been there himself. He was precise with the details, emphasizing the bloody bayonet on which the baby's body was silently impaled. A secret admirer of the Führer, that fool seemed to have every detail of his life on the tip of his tongue, and crowed that he kept *The Prince* and *Mein Kampf* on his bedside table. He calmly laid out the crimes committed by the trio, Nero, Daisir, and Juste Bertrand. He loved to recall how Nero had forced two brothers, one of whom was only seventeen years old, to first dig their own grave, then climb down into it so he could shoot them dead."

Antoine puts away his papers.

"You see, I don't need you to write your memoirs. Now the next chapter, which takes place at 476 rue des Hortensias, is of great interest to both of us, but first, I need a breath of fresh air.

Left alone, Rosa scans the room. A quick, silent inspection; her cruel, hungry eyes search everywhere. She struggles, tries to push herself up on her elbows. Her breath is heaving, like a whale or a leatherback turtle digging a hole in the sand for its eggs. She grunts, pushes, pulls. Like a hunted beast, she tries to get out of her bed, to escape from the hunter on her trail, driving her into the open. She arches her back pitifully, starts to sit up and then falls back again. The paralysis of her lower body seems to have gotten worse. For a long while, she grasps at the bed rails, clutches her mauve quilt, but all in vain. She can't make the pile of fat she's become move, not even a hair. Still, she persists, tries to throw herself off the bed. Does she think she can slither off and hide in some dark corner of the vast abode? Does she imagine reaching her arsenal, hidden away in one of her stolen armoires? Finally, her pathetic efforts get the best of her and she falls fast asleep, exhausted and full of rage.

8

Once back in the bedroom, Antoine sits back down in the same place, without even so much as a glance at Rosa, and, as if he hadn't ever abandoned his tale, he announces:

"Rue des Hortensias: My name is Antoine Guibert. In 1964, I was ten years old. I lived in Port-au-Prince, at 476 avenue des Hortensias, in the neighborhood called Bois-Verna. One Saturday morning, trucks filled with criminals arrived. At the head of the commandos, a woman. Her name: Rosa Bosquet. Not bad, am I right? But I'm not really happy with it. There's something missing ...

Antoine furiously scratches his head, thinks for a moment and then exclaims:

"I've got it! What's missing is the hatred—right? Hatred—that fervent and horrid determination that guided you along, Rosa, you and your band. How can I put that into words? How can I describe the irrational and blind hatred, describe the bloodthirsty, bestial fury?"

The other, still mute, yawns.

"Don't open your mouth so wide, it's really impolite and you frighten me. I don't like seeing those awful dentures. It makes me think of a crocodile, no, an alligator! They say they're more cruel. You're pretending to be sleepy so I'll leave? Abandon you to your demons? Because you're not alone, Rosa Bosquet, your demons are all around you, hiding beneath your bed, under your blankets, under your eyelids and your fingernails, in all the nooks and crannies of your rotting flesh. They're hiding there, squirming like vermin. They're with you, just as you have been with me, day and night, for all of these last forty years. How many sleepless nights spent in your company, Rosa Bosquet! In my dorm room when I was a student, I would talk to you, interrogate you, every night. So, here or elsewhere, we were destined to meet. Your voice, forever engraved in me, those phrases, always the same, coming back to me endlessly, the phrases that you spat out when your two hyenas found me hiding in the bushes. You see, I haven't forgotten a thing. 'Oh,' you exclaimed then, 'just what is this little half pint? This fetus? What's he doing here?' You had your hands clamped on your hips, a cavalier stance—quite vulgar, really—and I remember it clear as day. 'Clean that up too, right away!' My teeth were chattering so loudly, I was trembling so much that I bit my tongue and … even today I can taste the blood in my mouth. You read an unparalleled fear in my eyes—I'm sure you got off on it. My pants were soaked with urine, shit ran down my legs and into my shoes. You spat right next to me, then turned on your heels and were gone."

You need to know that I hadn't fled at the sight of the trucks. I was already outside the house. Little boys, maybe you don't know this, but they like to play in the woods. That day, I was in a little grove of oak along the edge of a ravine, the Bois de Chêne. I was there with a buddy, Joseph, Joseph Pétiot. We would go there to catch buntings, those little birds with yellow throats and tender flesh: my father loved them. I was trying out a new *fistibal*, a slingshot I'd just gotten, and I was thrilled at the thought of bringing home two or three of those birds to show my dad that I was worthy of his gift. One of those poor beasts had just fallen, hit with a stone. An untested hunter, I was standing there staring at the bird, his yellow throat newly stained red, when all of a sudden, the sirens and the first gunshots rang out. In a flash, Joseph raced down a little trail. Without even looking back, he took off along the ravine. And me, I took the path back to my house, forgetting the bird and my slingshot. In the distance I heard cries, howling, the sound of gun fire. Petrified, I kept moving ahead, as if in a nightmare, my eyes locked on those infernal machines, those tanks firing missiles at my house, which was disappearing, collapsing in a cloud of dust and thick, black smoke. One of your men saw me coming. He aimed his rifle at me. I took off, without really knowing what I was doing, and hid in the bushes. I was very small, you must have thought you were dealing with a child of five or six, but you were wrong, Rosa. I was already ten.

Hiding in the thicket and trembling from head to toe, while you were busy with your dirty work, I thought about the bird we'd just killed, Joseph and me. That bird died at almost the same moment as my whole family took their last breaths. I felt guilty for its death. That's how children are, Rosa. I was convinced that what was happening to me was a just retribution: they were taking my life, the lives of all those I loved, because of that defenseless bird, shot down to satisfy my father and my young hunter's pride. How I suffered because of that thought. Later, I often dreamed of that little bird. I'd see it splayed on the ground, the feathers on its breast trembling, damp with blood, giving one final shudder. And you, Rosa, did you ever once, even for one very short second, dream of the beseeching eyes of any of your many victims? Were you ever, how can I say this ... not inhabited, no, that's impossible, not haunted, either, that would be asking too much ...

Antoine pauses. Speaking now quite softly to himself, as he often does, his eyes vacant, his shoulders hunched, he goes out on the terrace, takes several steps, then comes back to the bedroom and turns toward Rosa.

"Were you ever revisited—yes, that's the word I was looking for—have you ever been revisited by the imploring gazes of your victims?"

He moves closer to the bed and stares at her fixedly, but seems not to see her.

"You are tired," he says, "me, too. I've been through the wringer! I ought to go lie down for a bit. But, while I think of it, how many years did you work as a torturer? Let's do the math: you were on the job when the unworthy Father of the Nation was at the helm; between fifteen and twenty years. Then, a little more than five years with his son, so maybe twenty-six, twenty-seven years all together. A full career, to put it mildly. You were barely thirty when you started in the barracks, Rosa, that's really quite impressive! To think of how young torturers are when they start on the job, and then to find them, after so many long years of work, their faces still fresh and smooth, no wrinkles, a few grey hairs, but still quite solid, resplendent, really. Should we conclude that, since crime does pay, it also preserves those who dedicate themselves to it? To learn that otherwise healthy assassins complete twenty-five or thirty years of service ... What a shock when you suddenly realize that they still have many good years ahead, and many other crimes to commit."

In a rage, Antoine swings his head left and right, shaking it as if he hopes that would give his head, his whole body, some relief. He wraps his hands around his own neck, hands that you'd have sworn came from somewhere other than his own body. He is struggling against some dark force, fighting against both Rosa and the monster rising within him. At that moment, maybe Rosa believes that her adversary is beaten—she must think he's ready to call it quits—but the interlude proves quite short. Antoine quickly regains control.

"You obstinately refuse to unlock your lips? Are you unaware that, in your brief moments of sleep, you speak perfectly intelligibly? Are you afraid of what you might say in your sleep? Is that why you're so determined to avoid sleep? Just keep on grumbling, fighting it any way you can. Me, like an animal hunting its prey, I'll keep watch and, when you do fall asleep, I'll be ready to pounce on any syllable that escapes your mouth."

When Antoine shuts the door behind him, Rosa gives a huge sigh. Surely, he's going to bring her something to eat, she thinks. An enormous vein pulses continually on her neck, which is stiff, as if someone had shoved a rod in it. She struggles to lift her arm and rubs her neck. Beneath her arm, the flesh sags, flaccid, like a disgusting teat, a deflated scrotum. Muffled sounds come from the kitchen; her mouth starts to water. Two small rivulets form at the corners of her mouth. Does she imagine herself in front of a mountain of toasted bread, thick slices slathered with fragrant butter? Does she see the papaya juice in an enormous carafe, shimmering with frost, or the egg yolk, a bright sun lighting up the plate? Her jaw clenches and twists, she bites her tongue and grimaces.

The door opens … Antoine, empty-handed. With a toothpick, he cleans his teeth. As if in a trance, Rosa starts to tremble, so great is her disappointment at not having anything to eat. She trembles so much that Antoine bursts out in ferocious anger:

"Stop play acting! You disgust me! You know, I've decided to wear gloves whenever I touch you, and you'll never make me feel remorse about it—that sensation horrifies me. In fact, since it's never too late to learn something new, here's a word for you: re-morse. Be careful, Rosa—forget etymology, the word doesn't mean bite again. Even beasts give their jaws a rest from time to time. Remorse is a throbbing, painful feeling: it cuts. Like a toothache, it's anguish mixed with shame, because you're aware you've done harm to another person. To be more precise, one feels remorse only when one recognizes one's error and regrets it. This is especially true when you fear that you'll get the punishment you deserve. Remorse, Rosa Bosquet, is something that harasses you, chases you, works you over, gnaws at and tortures you. It can also, like a plaster or resin, pull your eyelids back up to your brows and keep them open, night and day, wide open, preventing you from falling asleep. Do you understand? Remorse, it's what eats away at you like a dog gnaws endlessly on a bone! But you, Rosa Bosquet, nothing can reach you or move you, not make you shiver or even touch you; or rather, yes, there is one thing that touches and animates you, that breathes life into you: seeing another suffer, hearing them moan, wracked by the pain you are causing them; it's when you stomp on them, like you did on Mélanie's dog; when you drag them down, lower than any beast, just as low as you. That's it, Rosa Bosquet, that's what makes you come alive, like when you gazed upon that terrorized woman, Mélanie Brénus, and watched her swallow down, mouthful after mouthful, her dead dog—until she totally lost her mind. What animates you is to see a ten-year-old child, trembling with fear, teeth chattering, his mouth filled with blood, to see him piss and shit himself, to hear his silent plea and read that one word in his eyes: "Why?" What animates you is blood! Yes, that's what gets you off, you miserable woman, that's where you find pleasure. You think I'm a fool, Rosa Bosquet, or, maybe, like the cowards and scaredy-cats upset by my quest, you say I'm a lunatic! That's how you describe your victims, isn't it? Poor Laura, when at last she finally decides to open her eyes and to stand up to you, I'm afraid she'll just up and die."

The woman releases another of her dull groans. Her jaws clack against each other, the furrows in the mauve blanket grow deeper, but her shell stays intact; nothing will make it crack. Antoine gives a military salute and leaves the bedroom.

9

The sweet, fresh smell of chamomile wafts through the kitchen. There, in the silvery steam rising from the teapot, Antoine—eyes closed, elbows on the table—tries to pull himself together. He wonders once more what name to give to the series of hurricanes that ravage him whenever he's in Rosa's presence. Time is passing so quickly. Soon, he laments, he'll have to bring that monster something to eat.

Riiiinnng!

Rosa's bell, strident and piercing. Antoine runs back and finds Rosa just as he left her.

"Why did you ring?"

Silence.

"What do you need? I'm asking why you rang?"

Rosa remains mute, but Antoine, discerning a threat in her eyes, is filled with a savage rage. He grabs one of the bed posts and shakes it, screaming:

"Disgusting rattlesnake, you think this is a game? Well, then, we're on! No more bell, no more phone for you!"

With a quick snap, he pulls a snarl of wires from the wall, throws it all out the window, and heads back to the kitchen.

An hour later, he reappears, carrying the lunch tray.

"I'm bringing you more than you can swallow down, you dirty pig," he snarls. "In fact, you're giving me an idea: I could make you so much to eat that you'll die from it, what do you say to that? I'll shove a funnel into your insatiable maw to fill you up, just like filling a bladder."

As he talks, he sets down the tray, then helps Rosa to sit up and get comfortable. As she attacks the dishes, like a boxer in the ring, Antoine sits down to watch. Barely surprised, he watches her repeat the same scenario: without even taking the time to chew, she shovels the food down, as if afraid he'll take the tray away before she finishes.

"What a sow!" he murmurs. "I'll have to change the bedding again."

He turns away, but when he looks back a moment later, he almost thinks he's hallucinating. Rosa has stuck the plate on her face and, with her tongue slurping, licks it clean, then sucks on her fingers and smacks her lips. Antoine grabs the plate from her and starts to clean up the mess.

"I'm going to have to do this some other way."

His voice is as cold as ice. Overwhelmed by disgust, he wipes her face and then announces:

"Tomorrow I'll bring what I need to take your photograph, to film you during your meals. There are moments that need to be immortalized! They say that, back in the day, you liked to take pictures of your prey. It wasn't enough just to watch them suffer, you collected images of their suffering. So, tomorrow, photo session," he concludes, as he carries away the dirty dishes.

"As planned, we're going to spend the night together," he announces officiously when he comes back to the bedroom. "To pass the time during our long sleepless night, we'll see what's in your notebooks, and, of course, we'll write. I advise you, once again, to cut out your trembling act. I know that's part of your arsenal, but it doesn't arouse my sympathy. Although ... now I could be mistaken, because I have, upon occasion, been wrong, I'd even say ... willfully wrong about you, but at one point, my despair led me to believe that, during all those years, you'd acted in a sort of trance. I wanted to convince myself that you were suffering from some sort of madness that made you think you were the hero of a film, fighting for justice, a sort of Amazon tasked with cleaning up her country, ridding it of all who stopped it from working right; that you were only doing your duty, a woman motivated by the extravagant pretension of working for posterity! Standing here in front of your bed, right now, I still hope that you are lying, Rosa, that you're trying, for some strange reason—out of necessity, most certainly—to believe in a sort of angelic feminine spirit. I want you to try to pull the wool over my eyes. I want you to try to make me believe your lie, even for a brief moment, believe that you had nothing to do with it, that it was because of that clique, those men, all those dangerous fools with whom you consorted—eating, drinking, fucking—that you were transformed, little by little, into a blood-thirsty jackal. In the archival documents I found, there are vague elements of an answer ... Please allow me to leave you for a moment so that I can go get a few of those masterpieces and other bits of evidence."

Before leaving the room, he turns back to Rosa.

"Did you never think that one day you'd find yourself a prisoner to your past? A curse upon you, Rosa! Every day gives us proof that your victims can surpass yesterday's executioners, far outdo them in cruelty. Do the evil acts of the first end up imprinted, in indelible ink ... are they written into the very cells of those who follow? A curse upon you, Rosa Bosquet. This famous book that you claim to want to write, it will be written, but it will be nothing other than the transcript of your own trial!

As soon as Antoine is gone, the one that the militias called their "Dear Dragonfly from the Bas Peu de Chose neighborhood" fell asleep. A while later, when a noise makes her jump, she sits up and strains to hear. She thinks she senses a presence, steps, a creak behind the drapes. She pulls the comforter up under her chin, clutches it as if it had some magical power to protect her. Her heart jumps when she thinks she hears a familiar click. Could it be her Beretta, the one she got in Marseille, just before she fell ill?

The sounds of shuffling papers. Again, more steps. And then, a dry heavy thud, like a pistol dropped on the floor. Unless it's a knife? God in Heaven! Suddenly, someone coughs.

"You are who you are, Rosa Bosquet, you'll never be anyone else. You are what you were, and that's what you'll be until you die: a thunderbolt that burns, a jackal that devours, an alligator that rips, a hyena that kills for bloodlust! You are the stuff of all my fears and all my nightmares, you are the hell that has consumed my life, you are the sum of all my misfortune and all my rancor ... My hatred for you is far greater than hate!

Like a priest with a censer, Antoine bears an oil lamp. With slow and measured steps, he emerges from his hiding place, reading from his breviary of hatred. He turns off the overhead light, which heightens the glow from the lamp he holds up next to his face and the threatening shadows it casts. He comes toward the bed, turns off the bedside lamp. Rosa doesn't dare cry out, doesn't even dare move. All she sees is the glow of the lamp Antoine holds, illuminating his disconcerting face. He places the lamp on a coffee table and pulls it closer, then sets down a pile of notebooks, papers, a hammer, and a little metal box. Under his arm, a cardboard tube, from which he slowly pulls a roll of papers that he spreads open. Then he begins to pin photos on the walls. Soon the bedroom walls are covered. Rosa follows him with her eyes. Once he's set everything up, he settles down in the chair, almost seems to forget about her for a moment. He doesn't say a word, but feels the pain working its way down his throat to his belly, tearing a hole in his gut. From beneath lowered eyelashes, Rosa watches his every move, watches as he scans the photos pinned on the wall as if he were presiding over a reunion with all the ghosts he summoned. His lips move, he recites their names, murmuring prayers that he alone hears. He is dressed for the occasion in an immaculate white shirt, tightly fitting black pants and leather chaps. All of a sudden, he stands up. He moves slowly toward a dresser and picks up a pointer he'd left there. He lifts the lamp up to a photo.

"Look carefully, Rosa, at this man's face," he intones. "A high forehead, a frank gaze; perhaps a tad melancholy, thoughtful, but serene. You know his name, Antoine Guibert. Here, Gabriela, my mother. They say she had a fiery temper, passionate and, most of all, generous, expansive, a ray of sunlight, with a hint of the ingénue, for which my father adored her. Here, my grandmother, Gala, surrounded by her daughters. Under the watchful eyes of these people, who were denied a proper burial, we will write the book that will be your tomb. But now, onto other victims— among them, Ruth Emeri, the most precious jewel of the Bois Patate neighborhood. She supported her family, five brothers and sisters, an ailing mother, a father long deceased. And how she loved parties! At twenty, that's normal! As you can see, there are two of Ruth Emeri. First, here, dressed for a ball: a gown with crinoline, a plunging neckline, just ravishing! Beneath the picture is written, "Club Camaraderie, December 1963." How old was she then? Probably twenty-two or twenty-three. And then there's this one, your creation: Ruth Emeri, two years later, disfigured, burned with vitriol because she had the misfortune of being courted by too many men, including a certain Maximilien Adolphe, who was, for a long time, they say, the slave and plaything of Rosa Bosquet.

"Now this one, showing a young man's splayed body: naked, unrecognizable. The information gathered tells us his name was

Laraque. His cadaver was exposed, left to the mercy of the sun and the flies for several days. On the back of the photo, there's a short description: 'On the third day it was displayed at the entrance to the airport, the traitor's body turned from grey to mauve.' In the language of the executioners, victims are traitors."

"Look carefully, Rosa, another photo: two men, also about twenty. They are handsome, strong, well-educated. Their names are Numa and Drouin. People said they were generous. They were the future of the country, but today, they're not even remembered. They are tied to posts in front of a cemetery wall. Their eyes are clear, wide open; they are staring down barbarity and they will fall under the murderous salvos of your band of jackals. The shot that kills them will come from your accomplice, Franco Nero, who specializes, it seems, in *coups de grâce*. Go on, Rosa, explain it so I can understand: in the name of what holy cause were these young men assassinated? You and your acolytes, you forced schoolchildren to watch this execution. And now you will pay for that additional crime as well. For the frank gaze of these two young men that you extinguished on that day, you must pay, Rosa Bosquet!"

Rosa's teeth start to chatter violently; she struggles as if an army of ants had invaded her bed. She tries to stifle a hoarse cry as it escapes from her throat. Antoine raises the pointer threateningly.

"I forbid you to squirm like that! Be careful, that St. Vitus' dance is giving me an absolutely diabolical idea. I'm sure you scoured all the executioners' manuals, and so you know that since the dawn of time there exists one exceptionally refined torment reserved for stubborn old nanny goats. Old dried out bags like you get the sieve treatment! I'm warning you, it's entirely up to you; say the word and I'll set it in motion! Jellies, compotes, marmalades, molasses, honey, jams, syrups—everything, absolutely everything—granulated sugar, powdered sugar, sugar in syrup or cubes, everything goes in. You'll be coated from head to toe and then I'll leave you there, abandoned, buried in your sugary bed with ants and other insects, until they turn you into a sieve! Your sidekick, Nero, King of the Outlaws, excelled in this domain, bragging about preparing his victims for what he called a 'sugaring.' He concocted his mixtures himself and, with his bare hands, slathered them over his prey."

When Antoine wheels over a small table, Rosa is terrified to discover her whole collection of guns. She starts to growl and can't stop. Petrified, she can only growl. Antoine settles back in the armchair next to the bed and picks up the murderous objects one by one. He turns them this way and that, feeling their weight; he checks the barrels and loads them.

"Look, this Browning Pro 9 is pretty solid."

He pretends to be in ecstasy.

"And what detail you put in when you catalogued your little toys! Your notes are remarkably precise; congratulations! This one is a Jericho, that one, a Beneli. And here, a Luger, the only one I can recognize. What craftmanship! Real treasures!"

He sits up excitedly and takes aim at Rosa, who covers her throat with a hand, but is unable to make a sound.

Antoine reads:

"*Pedersoli Model Year XIII! Limited series of 200 for the French market.*"

He whistles in admiration.

"A real thoroughbred! And that's an understatement. Certificate of authenticity included, if you please! 'A wooden case with a lining of green Italian velvet, and a ceramic imperial medallion, the Order of the Crown of Faith, embossed on the handle,'" he reads. "You weren't skimping!"

It takes all of his strength to keep his cool. His tongue grows thick and heavy, but relentless, he continues speaking to himself, almost as if in a trance. He tries to find the courage to match his words, but exhaustion and emotion bring him down. Without another peep, he suddenly falls asleep at the foot of Rosa's bed. Like a drunkard, he crashes, vanquished, sad, and powerless.

When he opens his eyes, under Rosa's impassive gaze, Antoine bitterly regrets having let himself go like that, falling asleep in the armchair at his executioner's feet. Although still sluggish and half asleep, he realizes right then that Rosa is perfectly aware of just how ugly she is, of the disgust she inspires. He understands that her repulsive filth, just like her cries, are formidable weapons that she knows full well how to use, just like she used to use her strength, her beauty, and her pistols. He sits in the armchair, looks out on the garden, and mumbles:

"I must call on every last bit of courage I have to stay here, in this backwater, with … with …"

He hesitates about what term to use. He turns for a moment and scans the room, as if from somewhere beneath the furniture or behind the heavy drapes the missing words were going to emerge.

"… to shut myself away with such an ogress in this fortress."

Now Antoine is immunized against all of Rosa's spells, protected from her black magic, because he has nothing left, nothing but this empty expanse in the middle of which stands, like a tree that cannot be uprooted, his desire for justice. And over that empty expanse, over that desire, Rosa no longer has any control.

10

Another day. As fresh and bright as a reason for hope, the daylight floods in from all around. It comes from the sea in the distance and covers all of Gourdaix, rising like a cloud up to the rocky peak, and even penetrates Rosa's lair. Without Rosa, everything would be so nice, Antoine muses, everything so different. The easiest thing, he thinks, would be to just let it go, to leave: go far, far away from her, walk all the way to the sea, sit on the shore, sink down into the ocean, soundlessly, and let himself be swallowed up; disperse this madness once and for all. He looks at the still sleeping village. Beneath the clear sky, ancient roofs, clouds of birds flitting this way and that in the crisp, clean air, the farandole of laurel weaving along the walls around the homes, the flowered balconies, the little streets that tumble along through the rows of houses ... All of this brings one word to mind: innocence. But when the dawn carries along the peal of a child's bright laugh, followed by the cooing of a dove in a nearby tree, something else floods into Antoine—deception, perhaps, but also a sensation of heart-wrenching solitude. Heading toward the kitchen to make some coffee, he sees, at the end of the hall, the imposing front door, with its protective covering of gold-leaf. All he'd have to do is walk down that hall, reach out his hand and open the door, then he'd put the mountain and Rosa behind him, once and for all.

The morning passes, calmly, because Antoine seems exhausted. Rosa makes use of the time to rest. A little later, Antoine decides to head down to the bistro to see Laura. The afternoon is deliciously sweet, the air refreshing, and along the horizon, the lacy treetops are swathed in a golden veil. However hard Antoine tries, he can't just let himself take in this peaceful atmosphere, all the beauty that surrounds him; he feels lost and unhappy, rudderless. He pauses beneath a tree. As soon as he does, he is overcome with a desire to dig a hole in the ground and hide himself deep within. "Why did I struggle so to find her? Dear Lord," he cries out, "if you really exist, please show me the way. I no longer know who I am, what I am doing, or where I am going." What he does know is that the presence of a woman like Rosa Bosquet in this oasis amounts to an intolerable imposture. Once again, he prays with all he's worth for Rosa's death. Not far from here, there's an uninhabited region, just scrub and pine; he could take her there, tie her up, and leave her alone to await her death. A persistent and horrifying image takes over his mind: that of Rosa's swollen body, attacked by flocks of vultures that carry her away. Lying under the oak, Antoine tries to imagine how he would feel after putting Rosa to death. What is it that allows some people to give themselves over to crime so easily? he wonders. How can someone just go to sleep, night after night, and wake up each morning only to repeat the same murderous gestures, torturing and snuffing out life? Just what rage, what immeasurable fury, guides the assassins?

He tries to pull back from this dizzying abyss into which he falls, again and again each day, as he struggles helplessly, wildly, to make sense of the crimes he blames on Rosa, but it's no use. He'd like to be able to think of something else. He focuses on the trees and breathes in the heady, intoxicating perfume of the lavender that grows wild in the region, convinced of the scent's purifying quality. How lucky he is, despite it all, to be on this mountain where each blade of grass, each flower, each stone seems imbued with a life so pure, where everything comes together to create this great song, this great poem of life. Little by little, he is filled with a real sense of calm. That ball in his chest seems to dissolve, disappearing into the endless sky. He feels himself growing lighter and more expansive, strong—stronger, he hopes, than the monster he will need to fell. Spread out beneath the tree, he makes a wish: let the power of the earth fill him. Lying on the knotty roots, he slowly falls into a deep, restorative sleep, melts into the myriad living cells that shimmer and vibrate so passionately.

It's already quite late when Antoine comes to. He is chilled through, unaware of anything but the mysterious murmur of wind in the leaves. He has no sense of time, but he feels a friendly presence: Pablo is there. Did he dream of him? He hears his voice, wavering despite its youth, a voice broken by sadness. "Forget that chimera, Tonio. Forget it all, do not waste your time," that was his constant refrain. "That Rosa—just like the Pinochets, Stroessners, Mobutus, and others of their ilk who bleed their people—she'll die peacefully. And the next day, the day after, or sometime after that, people of good conscience will start to speak casually about the thousands of victims of those dictatorships; they'll line them up like so many candles, one next to the other, and then blow out their memory, extinguishing them for good."

It is only once Antoine starts to get up from his bed of roots and leaves that he remembers he'd planned to go see Laura, to explain that he'd taken the phone out of Rosa's bedroom. But there's no longer enough time to go to the bistro; he'll have to call her once he's back at the house.

Fears about how Laura would respond were eating away at him, so he was greatly surprised when Laura said, "I should've made that decision long ago, but I never had the courage. If I had, I'd be a lot less tired today. Sometimes she calls me up to four times a night!"

Laura also let him know that the new nurse hired for the day shift had already quit. Antoine could feel her anguish on the other end of the line. He hears her breath, coming faster, harder; just before her anger explodes, he volunteers to take charge of Rosa, day and night.

"There's no use, Laura, for you to worry so about finding nurses for the day shift; it's just too difficult. I'll take care of Rosa full time. If I get too tired, you'll hire Marie for a night or two."

Then he hurries to add:

"Just stop by whenever you can. After a while, we'll see if we need to make other arrangements."

The words thank you burst from Laura's lips: "Thank you! Thank you!" she repeats several times, before adding, "I am so grateful to you …"

Yet he can feel her hesitation, so he waits, patiently.

"I don't know when I'll make it up there," she finally admits in a quiet little voice. "I feel so tired! But you can always come find me at the bistro."

Before returning to his post at Rosa's bedside, Antoine pauses for a moment on the terrace. Another night had taken over the mountain, and Antoine, gazing up at the starry sky, is once again troubled by this paradox of beauty and horror so intimately entwined. That thought inevitably brings him back to his native land, which just heightens his anguish. He feels the anguish, like a chisel scraping away inside his chest. He rubs his damp hands over his brow, his face, then holds them up in front of his eyes and stares at them for a long time. How dirty they are, repulsive, sullied by the horror of those endless nights he'd spent imagining them digging into Rosa's throat. He goes into her room. With her eyes closed, Rosa seems to be resting, but she sits up slowly when she hears the sound of the door closing. He catches a glimpse of that fleeting expression of terror that always flashes in her eyes, but she quickly regains control and plasters a bitter smirk on her lips. Antoine realizes that Rosa has come up with one more trick. She has polished her weapons and hopes to gain the upper hand.

"You're trying to play the smart one, Rosa Bosquet," he says, "but destiny is aligned against you. You can't escape from me. I've taken control of your territory and am now master of your last refuge. There is no tower, no arrow slit, no rampart or palisade to protect you. From now on, I am the uncontested master here. You already know that Laura is exhausted. She won't be coming here again and there is no other nurse but me—me, Antoine Guibert—day and night."

Antoine begins pacing frantically all around the bed. He can no longer contain his rage; one moment he feels hot, the next cold. With shaking hands, he unbuttons and rebuttons his shirt. Finally, he decides that to calm himself down, he'll bathe Rosa. He goes to the bathroom, rinses his own face with cool water, then returns with everything he needs for her bath. As he sets to his task, he continues to harangue Rosa.

"You, who would celebrate New Year's Day by slitting the throats of prisoners so you could enjoy, in the most macabre of ceremonies that a demented mind could concoct, what you called a good luck bath for the coming year, mixing your victims' blood with champagne; today, you can't even give yourself a bath of fresh water."

He brushes the sparse hair on her head and, with a puff, applies a layer of talcum, then spritzes her with cologne. Blinded by his own suffering, Antoine unleashes an endless flood of words.

"You lie there, useless, slouched in your shell like a huge loggerhead turtle; even your soul is cloaked in armor. But your armor will have to give way, Rosa. Do you know that in ancient

Rome, a tortoise was what they called it when soldiers held their shields up over their heads to form a sort of roof to protect themselves from enemy fire? Where are your weapons, Rosa Bosquet? Your proud bearing, your cowardice, your malevolence, your accomplices? Who will protect you now from destiny's claws? In Latin, *tartaruca* means 'tortoise.' It comes from the Greek word, *Tartarus*, which we take to mean 'Hell,' the place of suffering for those who have earned eternal damnation. We should change your name to Rosa Tartarus; it would suit you better. Bosquet is too pretty. It brings to mind plants, wild flowers, perfumes, the scent of falling rain. You, the only thing you sow is death! You stink of death and your stench infects this whole region where you chose to set yourself up. To tell the truth, you didn't have to choose: a certain part of France clearly has a taste for the dirty remains of dictatorships. You're not the only one who's decided to live in this country, in this region. Bokassa and other swine got here before the big fat pig. When he arrived, the first night—I think it was in Grasse—this France of the Declaration of the Rights of Man was all too happy to welcome Papa Doc's son and his whole family, so happy that they made all the other guests leave the hotel where they decided to lodge those thieves! Money has no odor, no color, even if it's been soaked in blood; what counts is that you can show a hefty bank balance. The restaurants and nightclubs in the area all blessed this Duvalier manna! But if it continues to take in this dirty spawn, the region will end up stinking of blood, and the sometimes-cloying scent from the perfumeries will be supplanted by the abominable stench of rotting carrion!

"Hoooouuuuuuunnnn! Hoooouuuuunnnnn!"

Like the terrifying wail of a sinking boat's horn, Rosa's voice blares out. But Antoine, who no longer has eyes or ears, who is little more than an envelope filled with madness, barely registers the sound.

"I'll never stop saying it: books saved my life. I was lucky to have learned very early to love books and, most of all, to take what seemed to me to be the best from them. During my three years studying medicine, I did the same thing. I learned a bit of psychology, even if that won't be of any use with you. I took the time to learn how this strange and complicated machine, the human body, works. I know how to take life away, to extinguish it in a flash, like a flame you blow out brutally, or to sap it gently, bit by bit. You, since you were little, toads and lizards fled from you as fast as they could. It was Bérin, or no, rather his wife, the frail Mathilde, who'd sit on the veranda in the evening and tell of the atrocities cooked up by your already perverted child's mind. She knew you because you were cousins. I could never understand why Mathilde thought it was funny, why her voice was so gay when she told those macabre tales. She'd laugh so hard she'd cry, as she explained how, with some thick glue you'd swiped from the stand of Boulou the shoemaker, you'd stick lizards and geckos to a grater. Then, lying on your tummy in the dusty back yard of your house, you'd watch those poor beasts suffer as they tried desperately to free themselves from your infernal trap. They'd pull so hard trying to get free that their head would come off their body, their eyes still open in surprise, their guts leaving a bloody trail behind, guts shuddering in the dust. And still you persecuted them, determined to cut their guts into tiny little pieces, each one wriggling like a miniscule worm. My room looked out on the veranda. Some evenings when it was unbearably hot, Mathilde's voice would come in through the open window. She was trying to relax in the cool breeze—sometimes Bérin was with her. He often got angry at the stupid stories she told. One neighbor, Oscar Pérodes, and his wife, who for some reason was called Biscotte, sometimes came to join them. After the tales of *lougawou*, gangs of zombies and secret societies, would come the stories about Rosa; Mathilde's high thin voice would wake me up. Why did she so enjoy those barbaric tales? In her affected voice, those abominations sounded even more perverse. Only later did I understand that, had it not been for Bérin's careful watch—and especially Mathilde's fear of losing a man who, in this country eaten away by so much prejudice, had allowed her to climb the social ladder—she would have joined your band of she-devils."

"Oh!" Antoine suddenly exclaims, leaning down so close he just touches Rosa's face. "Look, there, at the edge of your worn-out eyelids, something is glistening: it's crystalline, clear, limpid, like drops of water. Are they salty? Jackal and alligator tears? What a strange mix! Is it because you are yawning? That would be some comfort. But there are also tears of blood. Yes, yes. There are those who piss tears of blood, Rosa—you know that. Don't deny it. Didn't you get trained in Managua, there in Somoza's barracks, where, under the watchful eye of instructors from the United States, they taught you the art of using a spoon to scoop out prisoners' eyeballs? I've said it before, Rosa, the truth will out. Besides, when you come down to it, writing your memoirs is just like the patient and meticulous work of an archeologist, bringing old stories to the surface. Some of them, of course, are quite current: the more things change, the more they stay the same, Rosa. The pendulum has been swinging at the same rhythm since time immemorial. Even today, people in many far-off parts of the world are experiencing the same torture, inflicted by people who look like you, executioners who know they can act with impunity and count on the cowardice of their fellow men. Your talents would be greatly appreciated, Rosa, in Guantanamo or Abu Ghraib. I can see you, tightening your wide belt over your fat belly, the rolls of your flesh drooping over your revolvers. I can see you, a smile on your lips, posing for posterity by a pyramid of detainees, naked and trembling with fear. To mark the occasion, you'd wear your shiny boots and your blue kepi, the symbol of your omnipotence; you'd lift your chin boldly, baring your protuberant forehead.

Right then, Antoine throws his head back and bursts out laughing, an irrepressible laugh, a laugh to keep from crying, which explodes noisily, spurting on and on until Rosa begins to howl to make him stop.

"Houuunnnnnnnnnnnnnnnnnn! Houuuuunnnnnn! Houuuunnnnnn!"

Rosa howls till she's out of breath, but Antoine just keeps on laughing all the more, his words lost in the unstoppable flood of his laughter.

"Bellow, bellow, my elephant, Rosa Bosquet, you cruel whale! Howl some more and show me your baleen! Open your maw, you ravenous beast, so I can measure the angle I'll need to shove the barrel of my rifle down your throat! Ah! Ah! Degenerate that you are, you don't know that I have my weapon ready to shoot you down! Do you think I'm a fool?"

He closes in on Rosa again. As she sinks back into her bed, Antoine leans down and whispers:

"Your arsenal is right there, but I brought my own weapon, a sawed-off shotgun, all shiny and new. Do you want to see it? Touch it? Caress yourself with it? It's like those you carried so proudly back in the day, slung over your shoulder. I got it just for you. The first and the last bullets have your name on them because, after I've shot you, I'll slice open your belly and bury it inside you. You so loved your little toys, it will be one last gift for you, your last gift, to take with you into eternity. It'll go with you to hell!"

Then Antoine launches into an elaborate dance around Rosa's bed. His overly long arms are the flailing wings of an exiled albatross in its death throes, an albatross alone and furious, abandoned by his fellows, abandoned by everyone in the Gorgon's lair ... His laugh, his cry of distress, fades away into an exhausted sigh and, as he falls into the armchair, he says almost inaudibly:

"Each idea carries me far away, but only to bring me back once more, like a shipwreck; each idea brings forth a hundred more, a torrential flow I have no way of stopping. All these years waiting patiently for this moment, hoping, digging through the embers burning at my heart. For forty years now, my heart has been eaten away, little by little, torn to shreds by bits of bricks and twisted metal, shards of glass, calcified bones, femurs, tibias, fibulas, ribs, and skulls, crushed, exploded by the heat, buried, reduced to ashes under piles of rubble and rocks. No more room for pride, nor for honor or grand sentiments; no more room for reason, either.

Dead to his pain, and frozen in his madness, the only sound Antoine can hear is the scratching of his pen on the pages he has started again to fill, furiously, passionately. The man is alone in that bedroom, stirring up dreams of flames, an upswelling of images from a ravaged childhood, the atrocious song of a country cut into pieces ... And suddenly, very slowly, like a prayer, a balm on his wounds, a poem emerges from his lips.

Like a block of granite, silence, with no vibration, no voice, no hand. Only the profound certainty of anger and anguish, a cold that grips the chest. And then, upon occasion, that infinitely sad gaze reveals a brutal nostalgia. The cry that never sleeps.

11

Laura's attitude had been clear from the beginning: she never called, never made her way up to the house to ask about Rosa. For his part, Antoine was sinking a bit deeper each day into his hallucinatory delirium. Laying out his legal case, he howled his distress to an irremediably mute Rosa and filled page after page of the piles of notebooks with his tight script. He told stories and explained, in turn posing questions directly to Rosa or taking her as his witness. Exhausted, at the end of his tether, he was nevertheless relentless, pushing her to confess her crimes and reciting lines of poetry by Cavafy that had kept him company through many sleepless nights. *Sublime and beloved voices of those who have died, or of those who are as lost to us as if they were dead. Sometimes they speak to us in our dreams. And for an instant, the harmonies of our life's first poetry resonate with them, like music softly fading in the distance of the night.*

One afternoon, while Rosa is dozing, Antoine slips out, returning several minutes later carrying records and books.

"I will speak no more, Rosa Bosquet. That's done. While I wait for you to decide to confess, you will listen to music. It's no use plugging your ears, I'm turning the volume all the way up."

Rosa watches in disbelief as he looks for an outlet to plug in the machine. Never had she taken the time to listen to music, except, that is, when she burst into studios to judge the compositions submitted in honor of the Supreme Leader.

"You'll listen to *Nabucco*, by Verdi," Antoine announces, holding up a record for her to see.

The Gorgon's body is wracked by spasms when the splendid and heart-rending music rises up in the bedroom, twice, three times, ten times. After several hours, Antoine comes back to change the record. Ima Sumac's intoxicating voice fills the room, expressing her joy and her will to live. Suddenly, the sound of the music makes something in Rosa give way; she howls out her madness, her cries demanding an end to her suffering. Rosa sees hell and falls into death's abyss. Antoine then gathers up his notebooks and turns out the light, shutting Rosa away with the two records playing on endlessly. He heads off into the mountains and walks all through the night.

Daybreak finds them face to face again. With her body shaking and trembling, her mouth dry, Rosa seems consumed by a fever, while the other paces back and forth, measuring out his words like prayer beads, emptying his heart of all the pus choking him. Antoine is now gaunt, his face haggard. A thick beard and bags under his eyes give him a somber air. How many days, how many nights have passed since his arrival? He has no idea. Time has given way to the weight of his hatred, and in this time, which is no longer measured as time, Antoine awaits the miracle that will deliver him from rancor and injustice. In one of the upstairs rooms, he discovered a small folding cot, which he set up in Rosa's bedroom. There, leaning back against a pile of cushions, just as she does, he stares at her and continues drawing up his case.

Since every story needs to unfold logically, I have begun with an analysis of the Alligator's feelings, her state of mind when she made the decision to put herself at the service of the Undeserving Father of the Nation. I have explained which avenue, which road she took to become one with the damned soul of that little bit of a man who assassinated our country. I have demonstrated how she climbed up through the echelons to reach the rank of Cannibal Queen. Over several long days and nights, I kept her awake. I hunted her down, questioned and harassed her—she kept her lips tightly sealed throughout it all. That's her choice. As for me, I just remember this old proverb: "As long as the lion doesn't learn to write, hunting tales will laud the courage of the hunter."

This morning the Alligator will have nothing to eat. She has stuffed herself often enough in her miserable life! Why should I worry about Rosa's hungers while I am wracked by so many insatiable hungers? Hunger for my assassinated childhood—the one that paralyzed me each time the teachers called out in class: "Bérin, Antoine Bérin, Mr. Bérin, come back to earth!" And I, my mouth agape, lost and ashamed, would face without flinching the teasing of the kids who did not understand my absence, why my mind had wandered so far away from them. They did not know that I was no longer a child, but one who had escaped from hell, a starving zombie that no salt could awaken. Several months after my parents' assassination, Bérin, that retired colonel to whom Rosa had sold me, decided to move, to change everything including my name, in hopes of doing the impossible and saving me. But, as soon as I was able to go out on my own, I found my way back to the rue des Hortensias and, each day, I'd wander around the edges of that open tomb. On the blackened soil, as if on an ocean of sand, I'd tread through the waters of my pain, walking hopelessly, picking up relics: calcified bones, bits of twisted metal, shards of bricks. As for my new last name, every fiber of my being rejected it. One day, with no warning, Bérin had said: "From now on, you have the same name as me, Tonio. You know that I love you, don't you? That's what's most important." I remember how his hand trembled, as did his voice and his eyelids, as he said: "Forget everything now, everything else, do you understand? Try to forget. It's better that way." One day, with no warning, I was no longer Antoine Guibert, but Antoine Bérin.

Colonel Bérin was a man destroyed by a silent pain. He had spent time and patience trying to tame me. He so hoped to earn my affection. Despite myself, I was never able to pronounce the two syllables that his heart hoped to hear, to consecrate his paternity—it was beyond my abilities. The most I could do was to call him uncle, Tonton, like his nephews. Rosa had demanded an incredible sum from Bérin to keep me. Because he had no children, but also because he'd quite quickly become attached to me, she had set the bar very high. Of course, this wasn't the first time she'd sold the children of those she'd had disappear. I'm sure she finds a way to make excuses for herself, even for that; she must say that she was offering those orphans a worthy home, or even that they deserved better parents. For a long time, I wracked my brain trying to figure out if I should consider Bérin Rosa's accomplice or my savior. To be fair, Bérin, who was working so hard to earn my affection, didn't deserve to be rejected. He'd often sit near me and take out his tobacco pouch. Slowly, precisely, using his one hand, and with a little help from his stump, he'd fill his pipe. Then, with his eyes half-closed, he'd ask me to read to him. For a long time, those moments were our only real connection. We'd read—me, because without books, I'd die; Bérin, because it was one of the only ways he'd found to get close to me. Knowing the fire that raged within me, he'd blow on my burns, trying to ease my pain: "Tonio, my Tonio, come back!" he'd say whenever I suddenly forgot the book, searching for some sign of my lost family in a cloud of smoke that brought tears to my eyes. "Tonio, can we keep reading?" An anguished voice that shattered against my triply locked heart.

As for Mathilde, Bérin's wife, she was, I believe, suffering from some mental deficiency. I admired Bérin's efforts to remain patient with her. Once—only once—did I see him lose his temper. That day, while she was repeating insistently that rabbits lay eggs, he said this: "Heaven took pity on the child who might have been born from your breast!" My only contact with Mathilde was at mealtime. Sitting across from Bérin, she'd pass the dishes, making sure that our plates were always full, while she nibbled a little of this, a little of that from hers, slipping one grain of rice at a time into her stupid little mouth, which she painted first thing in the morning the most garish red. She made sure my clothes were always clean and mended, just as she took care of her husband's, and spent her days in small-minded and petty squabbles with the servants, calling them awful names, accusing them left and right and in the most offensive of terms of sleeping with her husband. My memory of her is of a sort of sniggering ghost, a scarecrow covered in lace and gold plate, who went to mass morning and night. She was wild for chrysocolla jewelry.

Bérin loved me. But that was far from enough to let me forget what is unforgettable. His love, which I rejected with all my strength, only wounded me even further.

Antoine nibbles on the end of his pen and gazes out through the window into the distance.

"I ought to air out the room," he decides, "open the curtains and windows, it's so beautiful out. The sun always makes me happy. Despite you, Rosa, I love life. It is beautiful despite all this horror. Look!" In two leaps he is at the window. "Look, on the oak tree over there, there's a bird, a woodpecker, and a bit further, on another branch, a blackbird. Yesterday I heard it singing all day long." He returns to his tale. "It was when I was an adolescent that I discovered my passion for zoology. I started studying the relationship between reptiles and birds. Happy to see that there was at least one thing that could capture my attention and rouse me from my torpor, Bérin brought me all sorts of books on the topic. Birds are animals of the vertebrate class, warm-blooded tetrapods, with feathers covering their body. If we take a bird and try to understand its morphology, we can see that at the top of its head there's what's called the crown. Yours is entirely bald. After the crown comes the forehead and then the beak. There are different types of beaks, of course. The principal divisions are between the beaks of water birds, insectivores, wading birds, granivores, and birds of prey. You know very well to which of these categories you belong, you old monkey. Birds also have different types of feet: birds of prey have nails that form talons, like yours, and scales, a sort of rough skin that covers their legs. As for water birds, their feet are webbed, or sometimes have thick padded toes. And finally, there are perching birds, whose toes end with sharp claws. After studying birds, I began to research the complex processes of genetic mutation. But nowhere did I find the key to explaining you, Rosa. That's why I have no choice but to open you up and search through your guts! Down in the kitchen, just over the sink, there's a whole set of knives waiting for us, good and sharp.

Antoine pauses to stretch, making wide circles with his arms, before continuing.

"Today, you'll have nothing to eat. But I'll tell you what I could serve you: a big bowl of porridge, nice and creamy, flavored with vanilla and cinnamon, along with nicely toasted bread, a glass of freshly squeezed orange juice, two soft-boiled eggs with crunchy bacon on the side. Or maybe, maybe ... smoked herring topped with a sprinkling of parsley and slices of sweet onion, served with steamed green plantains, slices of avocado, as yellow as saffron, all dressed with a shiny splash of olive oil. Each bite melts in your mouth, delicious! Thinking about it, I'll make all of that just for me and I will eat it, sitting right here in this very armchair. After I've eaten, I'll tell you a story, the story of king named Tantalus. He had the bad idea of slitting the neck of his son Pelops and serving him up as a feast for the gods. For that he was damned to suffer in Hades from unending hunger and thirst, surrounded by water that fled from his lips and trees laden with fruits that disappeared as soon as he drew near. I'll spare you no details when I tell of his suffering, his lamentations, his remorse.

Three times over the course of that morning, Antoine describes for Rosa everything he could prepare for her breakfast. He finally just leaves, having given her nothing to eat. He goes back to his apartment, determined to get some sleep, but instead sits by the window, downing cup after cup of coffee and writing furiously. Although he left her room, he did not leave Rosa behind. In his frenzy, he keeps on speaking to her, calling out and questioning her.

Part II

12

Antoine hadn't had a chance to tell Laura about all the roads he had taken before getting to Gourdaix, hadn't told her of the destiny, the whirlwind that had brought him there. When, at long last, the reasons for his presence there became clear, he was already fully ensconced and, like fine powder, impossible to sweep away. With no fanfare and no warning, he had settled in, determined to upend, once and for all, that little corner hidden in the mountains and Laura's life.

Knowing that the restaurant is closed on Mondays, Antoine heads down the hill toward the village that morning to pay her a visit. No doubt about it, he concedes, as he nears the house with blue shutters, Laura must feel comfortable in this isolated corner. A huge, overgrown garden filled with blooms and, at the end of the path, oaks from a bygone era give the place the mysterious air of a lost island.

The dogs, always quick to snarl, didn't even stir when Antoine arrived. Laura was first surprised and then irritated that he could just waltz into her courtyard without rousing their attention. She was so stunned that she just stared at him without saying a thing when he held out his hand, the same long, slender hand, with a grip that hesitates for only the briefest moment before growing solid.

As soon as she noticed him, Laura had a sense of foreboding: something had happened to Rosa. For the past several nights, she'd had more of those strange, haunting dreams, dreams of a frantic, disheveled Rosa, who raced down the mountain in her nightshirt, the rolls of her flesh tumbling down and skittering like stones beneath her feet, and arrived, out of breath, begging her to get rid of that man. One more time, Laura lamented, she'd have to find another nurse. She could have made more of an effort, she could have gone up there one evening after closing, or during the siesta in the afternoon, she told herself repeatedly. But something—she couldn't quite say what—had kept her from doing that. Laura blamed herself, as well, for her lack of prudence. Hadn't she just welcomed that Antoine, and given him carte blanche, without even verifying his references herself?

After exchanging the usual greetings there in the doorway, Laura has no other choice but to invite Antoine to come in and have a seat. Then she offers to make some tea. A long time ago, she had made a choice to keep silent, a silence that fits well with this place, where she feels safe, protected from the dangers that she always felt circling around her. But then this man arrived—so handsome, such nice manners, despite looking like a castaway ... Little by little, fears had started to gnaw at her, but she'd quickly brushed them aside. Not until today has she tried to figure out why he'd been able to step in so easily, wondered whether she had entrusted him with everything or if it was he who had taken control of it all.

Put out by this unexpected visit, Laura makes the tea mechanically. She puts the kettle on to boil. Then she remembers that seductive smile plastered on his face the evening they first met. She begins her regular litany of self-reproach: "You weren't serious about this at all. Good god, you just welcomed him in that evening, like an old friend. It's all your fault. You can understand now why he feels entitled to just show up at your house without notice. He could have called; let you know he was coming. You've always been so naïve." Suddenly, another voice chimes in, Rosa's, sour and bilious, echoing all around: "All it takes is one glimpse, just a few minutes and, without hesitation, you just open all the doors and windows, release the dams and floodgates ..." Right then, a block of ice-cold metal forms in her chest. It slides around, careening from one side to the other, crashing loudly. Like a boulder carried away by rushing waters, it races down, tumbling and twisting on its path to her belly, to the deepest recesses of her gut, rousing moans of pains long buried; further and further still ... she's fifteen, then twelve, ten, eight years old ... always reprimanded, severely punished by Rosa for any little infraction—always somehow linked to something she's said ... Too many words, useless words, badly chosen words, forbidden, secret words, swallowed, choked back, buried. Voice drowned, memory gagged, strangled, crossed-out. Memory shattered, in pieces, in shards ... How can she heal after her words were banished? For as long as she can remember, she had to learn how to take hold of the reins, to hold back her words like one holds back tears: "Don't say a thing, do you hear? Learn to keep quiet! Do I need to cut out your tongue?" And that thing—the steely glint of a blade, the terrifying flash that makes Rosa's eyes spin—that always gave her the chills, just like the sharp bitter cold that floods through her right then. Even at just eight years old, she already instinctively knows that the shadowy threat that enflames Rosa could well be much more than just a threat.

Lost in her thoughts, she forgets Antoine and the tea she's supposed to make. On the stove, the kettle whistles frantically. Suddenly, she hears a distant echo:

"Laura, Laura!"

Startled, she turns around. Their eyes lock. She gives a vague, nervous smile and stammers in reply: "I forgot what I was doing, excuse me. I'll be right with you."

She sets to work, even as a storm is unleashed within her against that strange and unsettling man who arrived, out of the blue, and who, she is quite certain, will force her to face things head on. She ought to have taken Marie's warnings more seriously—she said she felt unsafe since he'd arrived. He needs to be out of here as soon as possible, she decides. She'll ask him to go. She just can't bear his presence any longer. She'll find some excuse, claim that she's tired. Maybe she'll tell him to come back another day, or better yet, just to go away, to leave altogether. She'll figure out how to manage with Rosa.

When she comes back with the tea, Laura senses that he has already guessed the words she has yet to utter. With slow and deliberate gestures—and feigned apathy—she places the tray with the teapot and freshly baked cookies on a little wicker table. Girding herself for an attack, she sits down in a rattan rocker across from Antoine, who is sitting on a bench. A look of concern flits across the man's face, like a dark cloud. He declares straight out:

"I won't leave Gourdaix until I get what I came for, Laura. That's the only thing that will bring me peace. I made a promise to myself; I promised them that I would find ..."

"Just what did you promise and to whom? What are you trying to find?"

Although left speechless by the sharp edge in her voice, Antoine doesn't lose his cool.

"It's a promise I made forty years ago to my family. It's no accident that I came here to Gourdaix—you've figured that out. I've been waiting years for this meeting with Rosa."

Laura jumps to her feet so quickly that her chair flips and crashes behind her. She stomps toward the well in the middle of the courtyard and perches on its edge, as if trying to reassert control over the space. Antoine follows, then stands defiantly before her.

"I came here intent on making Rosa Bosquet confess all the crimes weighing on her conscience," he says in a solemn voice.

Laura would like to give an off-hand reply, but her lips tremble, revealing the battle raging within her. She hesitates, torn between insolence and withdrawal. She opens and closes her mouth, then opts to follow Rosa's example.

Antoine hadn't foreseen this new battle front and so explodes: "Silence is of no use anymore, Laura. I'm going to use all my resources to bring down your fortress. Look!"

He pulls a piece of paper from his pocket and unfolds it.

"I have here a list of names, people who've agreed to talk about her, to confirm details. I need you and you have to help me! Please understand, it's not about hatred or revenge, at least ... I'm fighting for all I'm worth to keep those degrading emotions at bay."

"Neither hatred nor revenge? Neither revenge nor hatred ..."

Laura gives a strange, uncertain chuckle. Her eyes are filled with anger.

"Neither hatred nor revenge?" she repeats, before Antoine continues on in a leaden voice.

"Justice! That's what this is all about! Truth be told, I don't know what that term really means, but it's what I need," he insists.

"So, you actually believe in justice? Really?" Laura retorts, with feigned surprise. "You're just another idealist."

"Justice, human dignity—they certainly have no place in Rosa's universe. But what about you, Laura? Do they in yours?"

"Me? Yes, me!" she shouts. "Just what do you know about me?"

She stomps her feet, but when she speaks, her words are tinged with terror and fatigue: "If I can give you one bit of advice, give up your plan."

"Give up? Give up?" Antoine intones, clearly stunned.

That phrase clearly spurs him on.

"It's true," he cries, "there is no punishment that befits the crimes of Rosa Bosquet! There is no law that one can brand upon her flesh!

For me, there's only one choice left—for me, for us. Laura, we have to ensure that our own justice reigns supreme. The justice of two scorned beings, two whose lives she destroyed. Justice can't be an empty word! Justice must not be an empty word!"

Laura retreats once again behind her wall of silence.

Antoine continues, "When will you admit that you are one of the centerpieces of the whole structure?"

"I didn't choose this life."

"Why? Why didn't you ever try to understand?"

"All we have is one life. Mine is already mortgaged to the hilt. I spent it trying to catch a glimpse of the human being within Rosa, but that was a waste of time. And really, I've had enough of your interrogation." Her body stiffens. "Don't expect any help from me, do you hear? The past—it's dead and gone. And soon Rosa will be, too. As soon as she shuts her eyes, I'll be able to turn the page, once and for all."

She stands and awkwardly tries to smooth out the wrinkles in her skirt.

"There you're wrong, Laura. As long as there is life in me, as long as any of Rosa's victims are alive, the past will be, too. If we do nothing, we'll be trapped in this tomb forever. You must know that I'll end up getting what I want, with or without your help. By refusing to help me, you're just making yourself even more culpable."

"And what do you plan to do with the testimonies you're gathering?"

"I don't know yet."

"I understand. You're collecting them so you can write a book, right? You came here to get something juicy for it? You must believe that your writing will make you an agent of justice?" she continues, twisting her lips into a sarcastic smile.

That hoarse laugh reminds Antoine of how they described Rosa's. How many times had he heard Mathilde imitate that awful throaty laugh, just like a jackal's: bloodcurdling!

"You want to write the story of Rosa Bosquet's life?" Laura continues. "Why not just admit that's your goal, Mister Writer? You want to make a heroic gesture, flush out a prey all the easier to trap since she's at the end of her life. You shake your head, you deny it? So, what would explain your presence here? Given how old she is, just what are you hoping for?"

Antoine is not deterred by the question.

"Don't be so petty minded, Laura. It's no use. The circumstances in which I met Rosa are too painful. I'll spare you the details for now, but you can't keep on playing ostrich. Rosa is a criminal, she must face justice, because she is in full possession of her wits."

Laura closes her eyes.

"No, open your eyes, Laura! You have to be courageous, because there's no going back. I know that you harbor contradictory feelings about Rosa. You detest her and at the same time feel somehow in her debt, because, so you think, she took you in after your parents' death. Is that right? Answer me, Laura!"

"What gives you the right to come here and torment me this way? How many times do I have to repeat it: for me, the past is gone. And then, whatever she may have done, she's the one who was there for me when I had nothing else."

"Once again, there are many ways to see things, many facets to a story. Let me tell you a little tale, Laura, one that's very old, like all good tales. Five blindmen were touching an elephant to see what it was like. An elephant is a bone, said the one who touched its tusk. Not at all, answered the one who'd touched an ear; an elephant is a fan. Now, now, declared the one who'd touched the tail, an elephant is a rope. The one who'd touched a leg replied that an elephant is a pillar, and the last one, who'd touched the trunk, disagreed, saying that an elephant was intestines. You see, Laura, there are several ways to understand a fact."

"You have the gall to suggest you know my story better than I do myself?"

"Not only do I know it very well, but I certainly know more than you do about Rosa's, even though you lived your whole life with her."

"If I were in your shoes, I'd just leave," Laura protests once again. "I have no intention of taking part in your plan, whatever it might be!"

She spits out those last words in a voice bordering on hysteria. Her words fall through the air like a rain of pebbles. The old, limping dog grumbles out its concern, which is echoed by the two others. Antoine, who has no intention of leaving, leans back against the wall and waits.

My only day of rest, completely ruined, Laura grumbles through pinched lips. How many times did I promise to put a lock and chain on that gate! Had I, he couldn't have gotten in, she laments. She turns her back on him and heads toward the house. He follows closely behind. She spins around. They stare at each other in silence.

"Antoine," Laura finally says, "you are taking advantage of my patience. Just what do you have against me?" she cries.

"First off, you need to calm down. Despite what you think, I don't want a fight. I've been perfectly candid with you. I'm sharing my suffering and just ask that you help me to find some peace."

"What about me? Do you think I haven't suffered? Have I asked anything at all of you? Stop deluding yourself, Christ Almighty! Each one of us has his own cross to bear; life makes gifts to no one! Why did you come here to torture me?" she wails, on the verge of tears.

"I've been lost in a maze for forty years, Laura. I wander around empty handed, with nothing left at all but my determination to hear the woman who took everything from me confess her crimes, straight from her mouth. It's a dangerous obsession, childish even, as some have dared tell me. If I hadn't found someone to talk to today, I'd risk sinking into madness up there with her."

"I'll never be rid of you! So, tell me what to do, what you want from me. I'll do it just so I can have some peace!"

Despite the trembling of her voice, Laura seems sincere in her words. Antoine holds out the leather bag he's been clutching tightly since the start, although she'd barely noticed it. Laura grabs the bag and sets it on the wall.

"In that bag you'll find bundles of papers. Each bundle is a story. They're all different, but interconnected, and they all have Rosa Bosquet at their center. Open it. You'll find my story there, that of my family, destroyed by Rosa. And so many other stories … The packets are numbered and identified by the names of the victims and their dates, whenever possible. In bundle number 6, there's a part of yourself—an important part that you've lost. I have no way of knowing what will come of this. Is there any way I can spare you from even more suffering? I don't know. But look over the documents, Laura. As for what comes next, I'll trust your judgment."

He takes her hands, keeps hold of them for several minutes, squeezes them slowly. Laura feels the warmth and the nervous trembling of Antoine's hands, fatal and ominous signs of what's to come.

Then Antoine heads off, his shoulders hunched, without ever looking back. Laura feels her face grimace as a silent wail rends her body. For a long time, she thinks she still feels the burning sensation of the man's fingers on her palms.

13

He walks away down the long path. She stands, still as a mummy, and watches him for a moment. Her eyes blank, overwhelmed by a rising awareness of her own vulnerability. The sun is pale, its light filtered. It's late, she thinks, soon night will fall. That terrifies her. There's a bitter taste in her mouth; her lips are dry. All the strings that connected her to life are fraying. She floats, untethered, fears she might faint, turns her head for a moment to catch one final glance of Antoine, now little more than a shadow, disappearing into the broom bushes. He'll take the main road—it's longer, but a lovely walk. In less than an hour he'll be back in the grey house with Rosa. She should go in and lie down, hide beneath her down comforter, never leave her bed again, see nothing, hear nothing. Her knees begin to give way; she drags herself toward the rattan armchair and lets herself fall into it.

Laura stays there on the porch for a long time, curled up tight in the armchair, like an ailing child. Inside her, a blanket of grey fog. The sun has long since set, bringing an oppressive scent of thyme. She turns the same questions around and around in her head: should she call the agency and insist they send someone else? Demand that he leave tomorrow? He certainly won't want to go. What to do? She struggles out of the chair and seeks refuge in the house. Circling, like an animal caught in a trap, rearranging objects for no good reason, shooting panicked glances at the window. In the kitchen, she puts away the cups. Neither of them drank any of the citronella tea she'd made. She pours it all down the drain and heads to her bedroom. Grasping onto the door, she pauses, realizes that she's still thinking about Antoine's hands. Like a mirror that reveals the soul, hands hold a great fascination for her. What do Antoine's tell her? Tormented as he is, they are perhaps a disguise for a psychopath. A fleeting image makes her tremble from head to toe: Antoine squeezing Rosa's neck and howling, his hands kneading the soft flesh that oozes in thick coils, like clay. Rosa struggles, powerless, her eyes bulge out of their sockets, droop down onto her face, dangling by a thread of greenish slime.

Laura recalls the first time she met Rosa. The images rush by and she feels she is losing herself, becoming a stranger even in this place she'd taken such joy in decorating, carefully repainting each room ... She just has to close her eyes and it's September again. September, the start of school, a violent grief that returns each year. September, an endless corridor, the end of her life. Brown doors line each side of the hall. A strong odor of varnish. At the end of the hall, an immense door. In front of the door, Sister Emmanuelle, the one they call "my good mother." Laura and her friend Liliane say "the Chief," because you usually only see her when there's a serious problem. Sister Emmanuelle's face is framed by her headdress, a scarf so tight it looks like it's going to strangle her. A very, very white scarf. Her face, round like a full moon, her bright, shining clothes. So much white hurts the eyes. Her pink porcelain skin, like mother-of-pearl. You want to touch it to make sure it's real. Sister Emmanuelle reaches for her hand and then opens the door. They go into a vast room and Laura understands she's being led to the very back. There, near a little round side table, sits a woman. Photographs on the wall, portraits of nuns, all identical, with eyes like clear marbles. They're watching, as if sitting in judgment. Laura's shoes slip. In her legs, her stomach, the first tingling of fear—that she's going to twist her ankle and fall, splayed out on that overly glossy parquet.

The woman wears a black skirt, a polka-dotted blouse with a lacy frill at the neck. Try to understand how a mind works ... those details have remained engraved on Laura's memory with surprising clarity. She also notices the woman's shoes, so elegant: black with a buckle that looks like solid gold. Pointed toes, like bird beaks. Sister Emmanuelle glides silently over the parquet, still holding Laura's feverish hand. Her own is soft and damp. Laura looks up, her eyes asking questions she can't voice. Are there tears in the sister's eyes? Maybe. In that porcelain face, they look like they're made of glass.

"The bell will ring soon, Laura," Sister Emmanuelle says, her voice hesitant. "I'll go collect your books and your bookbag from your class. You'll be going home with your Aunt Rosa."

"My Aunt Rosa?"

Right then, the lady stands up. She advances, arms outstretched. Her fingers with long nails, red and shiny, are covered in rings, lots of rings. The pose of a statue. Gathering all of her strength, Laura tries to anchor her feet to the parquet. Her lips clenched, her fingers tensed, she freezes, grabs hold of the back of a chair: turn into stone, an immense boulder, a mountain that nothing and no one can move. The lady places a hand on her forearm. Soft and cold. A painful shiver runs up her spine, making Laura think of a slug, something slimy, a horrible frog. Her teeth clenched, she looks at Sister Emmanuelle, shakes her head left and right, "No!"

"Yes, yes, my sweet Laura," says the nun, her voice faltering.

She also shakes her head, and her veil slips backwards. Laura looks again at the woman, her nails, so red, so long. For a brief moment, she thinks the woman's going to drive them into her eyes. How to hold back the flood of tears pouring down her face? The woman opens the purse she carries over her shoulder. Click. She takes out a white handkerchief with a lace trim and reaches toward Laura's face—the girl pulls back. The woman holds the handkerchief out to her. Laura grabs it with a scowl. Not daring to wipe her nose with it, she continues to sniffle.

"There, there," says the nun gently.

Sister Emmanuelle's voice—a stream where words glide by, like water over stones, a current that carries her away—sounds muffled, as if cotton were stuffed in her ears.

"Your aunt says you don't really know her. I understand that you don't want to go with her. But, in light of the events, you must, my little Laura," the nun continues, trying to loosen the grip of the girl's fingers on the chair. (Long after this, Laura learned that the word *event* was the modest euphemism used to cover up the crimes and killings of the Duvalierist hordes.)

With a sudden glance at her watch, the lady advances with determined steps. She wrinkles her brow and places her hands on Laura's shoulders.

"It's getting late, my dear," she says, as if trying to imitate Sister Emmanuelle. "We must leave."

Her eyes fixed on the woman, Laura pretends not to have heard a thing ... Forget those words right away, I didn't hear them. I'm not her "dear," I don't know who she is, Laura repeatedly insists to herself. Or maybe, a vague memory, her father's voice one day, "Laura, this is your Aunt Rosa, come say hello." All women are called aunts, grandmothers, godmothers. This is just another, just one more, but her perfume makes Laura's stomach turn. She gave her a dutiful little kiss, barely grazed her with her lips, then immediately went into a corner to wipe her mouth with the back of her hand … Erase that kiss, the imprint of that overly perfumed skin. Clearly indifferent, the woman hadn't made the least move toward her. Laura had had to stand on tiptoes, stretch out her neck just to reach her. That is what she held against her most of all.

That meeting had taken place in a very large home surrounded by a thick hedge of oleander and camelias, white flowers with iridescent petals that shine like splashes of light in the darkness. Just as they'd arrived, her mother had remarked on the flowers' heady perfume; she loved camelias and four-o'clocks, which open their delicate blooms at night. There was a party in the house, a really big party with an orchestra. Fans hung from the ceiling, their blades spinning with a purr you could hear whenever the music stopped. Laura remembers being overwhelmed by the instruments, the brasses, the saxophones. The women, the swish of their skirts, made her think of dragonflies. Some wore dresses with slits cut high to the hip—Laura was shocked. They displayed their bare round backs, tossing their hair and leaning back as they laughed. Their extravagant gowns revealed their breasts. They were all wearing shiny shoes with pointed toes and high heels, like sharp bird beaks. The music was loud, but not enough to cover the loud, unctuous voices of the men. They puffed out their chests, laughing and giving each other big pats on the back. In their hands, glasses with cubes of clinking ice. People shouting to be heard, calling out to one another, others milling about.

Parties are for grown-ups. An unwanted guest, she wanders around like an intruder. She goes everywhere with her parents since her grandmother left. Like many others, Belle has gone away. The country is emptying out. A real hemorrhage, her father always laments, swearing that he will never leave. Laura remembers, as if it were yesterday, the quarrel her parents had that night. Her mother didn't want to go to the party, her father made the case that they had to, on account of someone named Rosa. All the way there, they had argued. Her mother was furious and her father seemed feverish, but mostly, very unhappy. They sat in chairs near the stage where the orchestra was playing, not budging once all evening. And the lady, Rosa, went from one group to the next, patting the cheeks of women who cooed when they saw her coming their way. The men embraced her, kissed her hands covered with rings.

In the parlor, Laura's fingers were still welded to Sister Emmanuelle's. The face of the lady calling herself Aunt Rosa is hard, emotionless. Sister Emmanuelle's seems to grow redder with each passing moment. The crystals of her eyes dim. Her throat tight, Laura sobs.

"No use shedding so many tears, Laura," the woman snaps. "Let's go."

Does she lean down and wrap her arms around her? Grab her by the legs and toss her over her shoulder, like a heavy bag? Laura has no idea what is happening. All she sees in front of her is an abyss, a black hole gaping wide, and Sister Emmanuelle's overly white skirt, a bell jar that will come down over her, that comes down hard. The round porcelain face bends over Laura and Laura slides, slides like a moon across the open sky, unable to keep from sliding down into the hole.

A melancholy night spreads out over Gourdaix. The heady scent of thyme and broom bush comes in through the open window, reaching Laura in waves, but it calms neither her anguish nor her bitterness, which surge in terrifying spasms. She sees the looming shadows cast by the big willows' drooping branches and those of the parasol pines at the far end of the garden—old familiar trees, faithful sentinels, constant and majestic, which now offer no reassurance. Who can protect her from those old pains? Nothing and no one, especially not silence. Become a cloud, the water in a stream, a petal, a leaf, stop trying to resist, just let herself die and be carried away by the wind. So many nights, so many long nights during which her lips murmured that same prayer again and again. She rubs a weary hand over her arms, her thighs. When exactly did she cease to exist? Why did life just pass her by, leaving her barren, like an island after a cyclone? Why did it carry away her blood, leaving her alone, assailed by pain, silence, and all of those absences? Laura curls up in her bed, caught in the memory she associates with the morning of her misfortune. Suffering is a strange phenomenon, she tells herself; we stupidly believe it will pass with time but, alas, no. The implacable flow of years does nothing to lessen our pains—on the contrary, they turn into indestructible walls, immovable boulders. Time had passed, nothing more.

14

The first time, the very first time that Laura woke up at Rosa's house, she was about to turn seven. A bedroom with blue curtains. Laura looks out through the window and recognizes nothing in the landscape spread out before her. In her parents' home, there is a courtyard, an almond tree, and another huge tree with very big leaves that rebel against the gusts of wind. But this house seems isolated. Hills all around. She sits on the little bed, and her eyes, still puffy, scan the room, pause on each piece of furniture. On the dresser, a picture of the woman who says she's Aunt Rosa, a photo of her wearing a cap and not smiling. On a low chair, next to the bed, there's a doll with curly blond hair, wearing a dress of blue lace that matches the curtains, her skirts spread out like a fan. The doll looks back at her with indifferent eyes. Laura howls ferociously and throws herself on the floor, pulling the sheets and pillows with her. She shivers and trembles, moaning "Mama! Papa!"

The sound of hurried steps. The door opens. She comes in. Is it still that same day or already the end of another? Laura wonders. She is there, standing before her, now wearing a different outfit, a dress with big red flowers, but still with that same intoxicating perfume. She ... the lady. With a hesitant voice, she says, "I'm here. Don't cry."

But Laura continues to scream, louder and louder: "Mama! Papa!" Still lying prostrate on the floor, she trembles, as if a powerful earthquake were ravaging her whole being. The woman's chest, her breasts, two enormous threatening teats peeking out of the neckline of her dress, come toward Laura. Are they going to crush her? The woman leans down lower. Is she going to kiss her? Scratch her? Laura turns her head away violently, rolls over, curls up in a ball.

"Mama! Papa!"

Out in the hallway, other steps, coming faster and faster. The lady steps back as another woman comes in. This one has a scarf tied around her head, like servants do. Servants always have scarves on their heads, Laura knows that. The lady speaks to the new one as if giving orders:

"Julienne, when you're done giving her a bath, let me know."

"Yes, Madam Rosa."

Madam Rosa. She's not her aunt. Laura doesn't want her to be, so she never will! The woman who just arrived scrutinizes her carefully. The scarf is tied low, just above her eyebrows, pulled tight across her forehead, concealing it. Laura feels her eyes on her, too close. The woman says:

"My child, my name is Julienne. I'm going to take care of you. Don't cry anymore."

Laura explodes. She shouts and stamps her feet. She'll spend the whole rest of her life crying. She storms and rages, howls till she goes hoarse. Julienne picks her up and Laura digs her nails into Julienne's warm arms, inscribing them with all of her pain. She doesn't have perfume on her chest, not like Rosa. She just smells of her body, a bit like a mama or an aunt, a real one. Still, Laura scratches her. Julienne gently rubs her rough hands over Laura's face. Later she learned to recognize the touch of those who struggle, who scrub, wash, and clean the homes of wealthier women.

"Laura," Julienne continues, her voice brimming with sadness, "please, my child, don't keep crying like that."

Laura stops scratching, but only to start trembling again and imploring: Mama! Papa! Julienne tries to undress her. She becomes a dragon, a tiger, a snake. She whistles, howls, tries to scratch Julienne again, or to bite her, to tear off her scarf. Yet something holds her back, even if she keeps struggling as hard as she can. Full of rage, she pulls back up the straps of the undershirt that Julienne is trying to take off her. She pulls, she pushes, struggling like a devil, not stopping until, in stunned silence, she realizes Julienne is crying, too.

Julienne leaves her for an instant and comes back with a cup full of warm fragrant liquid. She puts the cup to Laura's lips. Herbal tea. Laura drinks, because her throat is on fire. Julienne bathes her and dresses her in a nightshirt. Overcome by exhaustion, Laura lets her do it. Julienne feeds her as if feeding a baby, softly repeating these words, as if in prayer:

"Eat, my little one, my child, open your mouth! Eat so you can sleep, eat to make me happy."

Laura doesn't want to sleep. Nor does she want to make Julienne happy, because she lives in Rosa's house. So, she's surprised when she does open her mouth and swallow the rice pudding with milk and raisins that stick to her teeth. She swallows it down to fill the gaping hole that has opened up inside her, swallows without even chewing. A light touch of lemon zest and cinnamon, a scent that reminds her of her mother. She wonders where her mother has gone. She doesn't ask Julienne—she wouldn't know. Her tears start to fall again, her nightshirt is already soaked. Tears roll down her neck, seep into her mouth, blend with the spoonfuls of rice pudding. What good would it do to ask where her parents are? Julienne already told her she doesn't know.

"Madam Rosa will tell you, little one. Me, I know nothing."

A first heartbreak. Immense, like the tallest of mountains. Laura feels so weak, her eyes grow heavy. To distract her, to make her forget, Julienne tells a story, the story of *Maman dlo*, the Mother of the Waters.

"You'd think she was a witch, because her back is covered with scales, her mouth, full of rotten teeth. Her grey hair hangs like ropes and her breasts, two empty bags, droop down to her knees. But you've got to be careful: Maman dlo is a fairy. She is kind and rewards good little girls by granting their wishes, even those that seem impossible."

Then Julienne tells her that she was only five years old when her mother, who was very poor and couldn't feed her anymore, took her to live with a lady.

"Mama was sad, but she told me: 'The lady will be able to send you to school. She promises.' That was a lie. She made me sleep under a table in the chicken coop. I had to take care of the whole house, fetch huge buckets of water, and I never went to school. I was lucky that Maman dlo was watching out for me. She went to my mother in a dream and warned her, so that one day my mother came back to get me. You'll see, little one, if you are good, Madam Rosa will take good care of you, and besides, Maman dlo is watching over you."

Laura is nodding off. Julienne gently tucks her in bed. Laura begs Julienne not to leave, because she's afraid of everything, of Maman dlo, and, most of all, of the lady, with her nails and that voice ...

"I'm afraid of Madam Rosa," Laura stammers.

"Don't be afraid, little one, and don't forget, Maman dlo is watching over you."

Heartbreak and exhaustion win out over rebellion. When she wakes up, Laura finds Julienne at the foot of her bed. She's wearing a different scarf, a different dress, too. Like a marionette on strings, Laura obeys. Julienne washes her, dresses her, does her hair. Then, holding her hand, she leads her to a dining room. Rosa is there, with her nails just as red as the day before and curlers on her head. She's drinking coffee. Laura wishes very hard that she might burn herself—wishes with all her might. Once again, Julienne feeds her—buttered bread and a bowl of porridge. Laura doesn't like the porridge, it's like glue. With each spoonful, she thinks she's going to choke. The cinnamon and star anise are roaches swimming in that pasty, greyish mush. Madam Rosa tells Julienne to let her feed herself. Julienne obeys. Laura doesn't like the porridge, but still, she eats it. With a huge sob caught in her throat, she swallows it down. Maman dlo will be proud, she'll warn her mother that she's dying.

"Mama! Papa!"

She explodes like an over-filled balloon. She spatters the whole table and even Madam Rosa's head. The lady drops her cup and lets loose with a sharp cry: "Julieeeeeenne!"

The maid comes running. In a panic, she grabs Laura by the hand and drags her off to the kitchen, where she cleans her up.

"That wasn't nice, you know."

"But ... it just happened. I don't like that porridge."

"From now on, you have to eat everything that's put in front of you, little one. You know there are lots of children who don't ever get anything to eat? Do you know that?"

"No."

"Well, one day, I'll show them to you. A big swollen belly, like this"—she cups her hands in front of her stomach—"their hair red and dry, like coconut straw, legs like matchsticks, eyes full of pus. They cry all the time because they're hungry, the flies circle around their faces, and they can't do anything to swat them away, they're just too weak to even move."

Julienne's voice is filled with anger. Laura is surprised, although she senses that she's not angry at her. Still, Laura is suffering too much to feel ashamed. After washing her off, Julienne hugs her tight. She caresses her tenderly, as if asking for forgiveness. With a big sigh, she continues:

"Maman dlo won't be happy if you act like that again."

"I want my mama."

"It's my turn to talk now, Laura."

They hadn't seen her come in. Rosa is no longer wearing her awful red robe. She's taken out the curlers and pulled her hair back. That hairdo makes her eyes look like stones ready to come out of their sockets. Laura would like Julienne to ask the lady to leave her alone, but Julienne is petrified. She quickly picks up the dirty towels and rushes out of the kitchen. Laura's heart breaks as she watches her go. Rosa places a hand on Laura's arm. The girl begins to tremble again. She trembles so much that the woman wrinkles her brow and touches the girl's forehead.

"Do you have a fever?" she asks, then answers her own question. "No, I don't think you have a fever."

Laura has no idea. When she has a fever, her mother just puts her hand on Laura's forehead, and that takes care of it. The fever is gone. She's so terrified her teeth begin to chatter. The woman looks worried. She puts a hand into her pocket, jingles her keys and decides, "Today, you won't go to school. Julienne will take care of you."

She pauses for a few minutes, watching Laura as if she didn't know what else to say. Suddenly, she raises her voice. She wants to be sure that Laura hears each and every word:

"I came to talk to you about your papa and your mama."

The child's heart leaps. Her eyes filled with hope, she waits. The woman tiptoes across the kitchen and closes the door. She comes back, pulls out a chair and sits down. She fidgets with her fingers and her rings, rubs her hands, then takes hold of Laura's and says:

"You parents know that you are suffering, but they don't want you to cry. They have asked me to take care of you."

Laura feels her legs turn into cotton.

"They've left for *Zetazuni.*"

Laura opens her eyes wide and pulls her hands away.

"*Zetazuni,* that's New York," the woman clarifies. "You know, where Belle lives."

Belle, that's her maternal grandmother. So, Laura tells herself, my mother leaves me to go be with her own mother. With no warning, she leaves me in the hands of some stranger with nails like claws. And my father goes with her, just abandons me, too. She's thunderstruck, completely lost, so angry at her parents that she doesn't even think about crying anymore. Something powerful and unrelenting begins to grow within her, displacing her heartbreak. The woman continues speaking, but Laura barely listens.

"They'll write to you and explain everything. You'll see, they'll send you lots of beautiful things. You understand, you understand they couldn't leave you alone?"

The despair that grows within her is beyond compare. Trapped in a bubble, her whole being stiffens. Determined and ferocious, she refuses to be mollified. The woman is talking, but Laura hears nothing. She makes threats, but Laura doesn't even notice. Her heart, drowned under waves of hatred, has ceased to exist. She rejects all compassion. This is her torment: the deathly horror seeping, drop by drop, through her veins and taking over her soul is all she has left. She is nothing but a ball of intense hatred.

Laura knows that several little girls in her school have a mother or a father, often both parents, who have gone. Everyone goes away, it seems, to *Zetazuni*. Because of that, some of them sleep at the school. They stay there all the time because they no longer have a home, no more parents. They're called borders. They comfort each other each Sunday by showing off the extravagant dresses they receive from overseas. They have necklaces, bracelets—charm bracelets with their names engraved on them. They wear socks and underpants with lace ruffles from *Zetazuni* that they show off happily whenever they run and climb on the monkey bars. They're also sent dolls—often even bigger than they are—with blond hair and blue eyes.

"Of course," continues the woman, who Laura refuses to look at, even though she keeps asking her to, "I'm going to love you just like your mama. I will be both your papa and your mama, don't ever forget that."

She waves her hands as she speaks, and all Laura can see are those nails, red and sharp.

An overcast day rises over Gourdaix. Worn out and exhausted, Laura is as grey and grim as the clouds that began gathering at dawn and have grown into menacing black masses. The stormy weather gives her an unexpected pretext to stay in bed, where she's been hiding for the past two days, drained, powerless against the flood of memories. "I have lived like a fugitive, tracked by dogs," she says to herself. "Memories like mastiffs, ghosts nipping at my heels like bulldogs. I'd always hoped that, once Rosa was gone, I'd finally enjoy some peace, but here comes Antoine, another beast who's got me in his claws."

There's nowhere for Laura to hide. Then a burning sense of injustice floods through her. "It's too easy, I can't, I must not let him do it," she repeats in exasperation. Suddenly, she jumps out of bed and starts shouting; the violence of her cries frightens her. Has she become that mad woman who nursed her anger for years, hiding in the shadow of the mountain? Let her rage explode, yes, come crashing down ... but aimed at whom? "Against whom? Against whom?" Laura chants. Overwhelmed by her own powerlessness, she blindly throws knickknacks, dishes, frames, and plants out of the window. "Against whom can I unleash my hatred? Against Antoine, against Rosa?" She collapses, spent, out of tears and fury. There are no answers to her questions. Julienne had made her understand that from the moment she arrived at Rosa's.

15

It took Laura several days to get over her reticence and find out just what was in the dossiers Antoine had given her. That inventory of the crimes and abuses committed by Rosa and her stooges was impressive. Everything had been recorded, down to the smallest details—carefully, meticulously annotated by Antoine. In numbered envelopes, she found newspaper articles, speeches, orders for executions, massacres. Laura felt trapped by those papers, by the horror they inspired and also by fear. How to escape it all?

Days pass and nights fall. Another day, another night … One morning, the sun is still low in the sky. The mist that shrouds the treetops in the distance is growing before her eyes. But Laura knows it won't last long. The sun will end up burning through, it will vanquish the swath of grey, she tells herself. Just the opposite with the shapeless mass of heartbreak and pain growing ever thicker within her, dogging her relentlessly. In her room there is no watch, no clock; she hasn't the strength to go to the kitchen and check the time. And besides, what does time or even weather matter—she's not hungry, not thirsty. She feels nothing but a limitless void. No more daily routine, no day, no night.

How many days has it been since she barricaded herself in her house? Three, four … she has no idea. She didn't even put up a closed sign on the bistro door. She simply isn't there anymore. She manages to feed the dogs somehow, and munches now and again on a cookie, drinking nothing but tea. Nothing, absolutely nothing manages to rein in her feeling of being set adrift, that sensation of losing her footing, of no longer being able to hold onto the persona that Rosa somehow crafted for her, an incoherent mix of a ferocious child and an adventurer—that persona within her who fills her with disgust and who must die.

Since Antoine brought her the dossiers, she's hidden in her bed, diminished and lethargic. Trying to pull herself out of it, she starts circling around the house, armed with a broom and dust cloths. She goes back and forth, murmuring, sweeping, dusting, throwing out with barely a glance an impressive number of things, seeking to erase a stain that won't go away. In the evening, she takes endless baths, scrubbing herself with a sisal cloth, as if trying to take off her skin. She'd thought that in the calm of this village she'd succeeded in protecting herself from life's claws, but Antoine's arrival unleashed in her an unfamiliar and unbearable feeling.

Then comes a day when she feels a need to move that she cannot ignore, a need to calm the anger and despair that flood over her in waves. Like a paralytic who learns to walk again, she slowly makes her way down the main road toward the village. She walks for a long while, wandering wherever the road and her feet take her, pausing like a beggar to stare with unseeing eyes at the walls around the castle in Gourdaix, lingering in front of the many stands set up by the artisans who reside up and down the hilly little streets. She wanders like that until evening, searching on each façade, behind each door, for some refuge, some sign that might save her.

The first rush of spring hints at the summer to come. Laura feels the sap starting to rise, a certain violence in the air and, suddenly, within her, too, the same impetuousness, the same need to move. It's all mixed up inside her, even the scents of the flowers. The heady, sweet perfume of lilacs is everywhere, as if the flowers, having waited too long, finally exploded. But to her it smells of rot, of the beasts who died of hunger last season and now lie in the thickets. The wind rises up. Tree branches sway furiously, as if trying to break free from their trunks, liberate themselves from their roots. Dusk is falling. Laura sinks down onto a bench. A dog comes up, sniffing all around. He ignores Laura and wanders away. Soon it will be night. She has walked all day in search of an answer, some consolation she will never find. Several times she tells herself she ought to climb up there, go see Antoine, admit that she has known who Rosa is for quite a long time, that she knew about the burning down of the house. She had heard about it one evening, when Rosa was in heated discussions with her assistants. She also knew other details, about other murders crammed in

Rosa's memory. But is it even possible, as far as Rosa is concerned, to talk about memory? She truly doubts that those crimes ever come to haunt Rosa. And then, as human beings, don't we have some control over our memory? Can't we select what should be crammed into it or not? Isn't that just what she had actually done, making accommodations, despite herself? A shameful betrayal of her soul. A voice, buried deep within her, snaps back, "That was the price of survival, Laura. Where would you have found the strength to build a new life for yourself?" Frightened, she looks around her. Always that same voice ... ever since the day when she understood that her life and Rosa's were bound together and that no land would be big enough to contain all the hatred she feels for Rosa.

Relentless, the voice hammers away: "Why didn't you run away ... far away from her? You're just one of those people who thinks they can live without making choices. When you sat on school benches alongside the children of executioners, courage had already abandoned you ... You in some sense belonged both to the executioners and the victims. That's how human beings are molded, isn't that right? Very early on, they are broken, transformed into a dough, and set side by side, where they lean over the same books, play the same games, breathe the same breath: children of executioners, children of victims. The nuns knew, just like those venerable monsignors who hid weapons under their cassocks and joined all the others at those Thursday dinners, lining up to receive their pittance from the *reines-choches*: bundles of clothes, packets of provisions, treats prepared just for them in exchange for the lists of the members of their flocks ready for slaughter!"

It's starting to get chilly. Laura lies down on the bench. I'll just let myself die right here, she thinks, die looking up at the sky. That will be nice. Tomorrow, at dawn, those who come to pick up the garbage abandoned by the night will carry me away. Once again, she catches herself starting to unwind the thread of her life. She thinks of that part of her childhood in Julienne's skirts. Julienne, who, despite the poverty in which she'd always lived, never had anything but words of hope on her lips. Where ever did she find the strength? Laura still has no idea.

Sleep is lurking, waiting for her, so she gets up and starts off to join Antoine. First, she stops at her house, goes down to the cellar and comes backs with a metal box. She puts out a fresh bucket of water for the dogs, fills their food bowl, shuts the windows and doors, as if she were leaving on a long trip. Holding the box in her hands, she heads toward Rosa's house.

Antoine was waiting for her. He leads her into a bedroom where everything seems ready for a ceremony. He pulls the curtains closed, helps her to sit on the bed. Incense is burning in a dish, filling the air with a calming blend of rose and lavender.

Perched on the edge of the bed with the metal box on her knees, Laura looks gaunt, like a hunted beast. Struggling to breathe, she looks around, as if trying to find a way out. Antoine walks toward her, his arms outstretched, and receives the box as if it were a religious relic. Then suddenly, awkwardly, hopelessly, she stretches her body toward Antoine, tries to hold him back, to take back what she just gave him: the box and what it contains. She wants to tell him that she was never able to read through to the end, never had the courage to examine all the documents in it, to learn everything there was to know about Rosa. She also wants to tell him about her life in France, her hopes, how she's been waiting, madly, for Rosa to die, and the desire she constantly represses to hasten her death, to let her perish or strangle her. But she will say none of that. Because of the wall blocking her throat. How can she bring it down? Instead, she lies down and almost immediately falls into a deep, heavy sleep, as if she knows Antoine will watch over her.

Antoine carefully pulls up the sheets around her, tucks her in like a child. She sleeps soundly, as she always has, with her fists clenched so tightly that in the morning Julienne would carefully wash her palms to soothe away the marks left by her nails. With the covers pulled up beneath her chin, Laura sleeps, stock still, no more than a body long ago surrendered to the night.

Abandoning his post at Rosa's bedside, Antoine drags his bed into the hallway. On the left, the bedroom where Laura sleeps. Between the two rooms, Antoine, like a jailer counting the hours. Now that he has found his torturer, that he is shut away with her in the same house, breathing the same air, sleeping at the foot of her bed; now that he knows that this torturer will never express the least regret, what is he going to do? Earlier that day, locked away in the bathroom, Antoine had cried like an abandoned baby. He'd looked in the mirror at his greying temples, the growing bald patch, the sagging skin on his neck. Rosa, he laments, stole

almost fifty years of my life. This quest is over; what will I do
with the years I have left? he asked the mirror. What will ease my
pain? How will I find freedom? The night before, he had given a
long speech to Rosa about freedom; he said he was giving her the
chance to take a step toward freedom by repenting her crimes. A
flash of lucidity? At a certain moment he thought he saw a shadow
of sadness in Rosa's eyes. He'd come closer to the bed, handed her
a block of paper and a pen.

"Here," he'd said, "take this paper, Rosa. Write that you're sorry.
Ask for forgiveness."

Emotionless, Rosa just stared at the things with dry eyes. Then
Antoine went back to his bedroom to get a new record, an endless
ode to freedom by Irène Papas. He set the player once again on
repeat and then shut the door behind him.

Dawn is just blue-tinged tenderness, as if the sky's anger had finally
given way. Antoine went out to walk, to release his demons and his
fury in the fresh morning air. Each morning, as he walks among
the trees and over that rocky peak, Antoine gathers his forces to
confront the beast. He leaves early, heading down the sloping
streets to the heart of the village, sometimes bringing back fresh
bread and brioches that he barely eats and ends up feeding to the
birds. He passes the Sainte-Paix chapel, contemplates the walls of
pink and grey stone as if seeing them for the first time, goes by the
park and the castle's hanging gardens, continues along to Victoria
Square and the main road. He can name each of the stones on the
path, he knows all the trees in Gourdaix, his steps are engraved,
each day a little deeper, on the fern-covered paths, the same ones
he'll take when he walks back up the same little hill covered with
heather and lavender. He stops every day under the same tree to
write out his case, convinced that Rosa must answer for her acts,
her crimes against humanity. He has gone through hundreds of
documents about the famous Nuremburg trials. The more sources
he gathers, the deeper his questions about the value of those trials
and the justice of mankind. How can one believe in morality
when the courts of justice are tools that serve the powerful? That
morning, he scans an article about the International Criminal
Court, which, it says, is just one more hastily thrown together
parody of justice. "*These tribunals,*" the article concludes, "*are tools,
like so many others, that serve political interests.*"

A brutal vision shakes Antoine: that of Rosa, standing, one hand placed on the Bible, proclaiming herself not guilty. A shock runs through him—attention! Voices rise up, reverberate within him. It's not him, but rather his blood, the blood of all those who died, a torrent of anger, that bursts from the mountain and shouts: "Death to the Alligator!" Antoine wants to flee, to plug his ears so he cannot hear the din, but the new growth of ferns beneath his feet and the endless buzzing of insects in the shrubs all clamor for his attention, amplifying the rumblings for justice that are urging him on. Everywhere all around, the same thirst for renewal. Everywhere, things are on the move, he tells himself. But when he starts off along the path that leads back to the house, the clamor pursues him, grabs on to his shirttails, rings his neck: "Death to the Alligator!"

Antoine opens the door to the bedroom where Laura is waiting. He is suddenly struck by something in her, something he hadn't noticed when she arrived. In a flash he understands that she has decided to make a clean break. She reaches out her hands to him. He helps her to stand, goes with her out onto the terrace, offers to make her breakfast. She only takes tea, which she drinks with both hands wrapped around the cup, warming her swollen fingers. A flock of birds suddenly lands at the foot of a tree, happily pecking away at last summer's cherries, which have dried on the carpet of moss and grass. Life is right there, but Antoine and Laura are not. Side by side, they stand, orphans with nothing and no one left but their memories. Antoine watches her drink. He waits. He's used to that—his whole life has been a painful and exasperating wait.

Until the end of his days, he'll hold on to the memory of the day he stood before the tribunal to receive the document certifying the return of his name. He loved to call it his "rebirth certificate." When Bérin died, he had undertaken the long and arduous process of reclaiming his father's name. His heart was pounding so hard when he heard the bailiff's voice over the loudspeaker: "Monsieur Antoine Guibert, Antoine Guibert. Calling Monsieur Antoine Guibert," that he, who'd waited so long for that joyful moment, couldn't answer. He was frozen in place, sitting stock still, unable to make a sound, and the bailiff had called someone else. He'd had to wait several more hours before approaching the desk, just as the office was closing.

Laura's voice broke the silence.

"Do you know why I'm here?"

"I think so ... Still, I'd like to hear you say it in your words."

"So I can stop trembling," she begins. "I read this sentence somewhere in a book, in the Bible, I think, 'I tremble in my bones.'"

"That's from the Book of Job," Antoine explains. "The exact phrase is, 'Fear came upon me, and trembling, which made all my bones to shake.'"

"Yes, that's it," Laura confirms. "It's time for me to be cured of this ailment. I tell myself that maybe ... maybe I should give myself another chance. Maybe by joining in your search, I'll finally be able to rid myself of this burden."

"Thank you is too humble a word for the circumstances, Laura ..." Antoine's voice cracks. "I'd like to shout my joy from the rooftops," he finally murmurs ...

The emotion conveyed by his words unsettles her, so Laura bows her head and interrupts him, asks whether he's been able to go through the contents of the metal box.

"No, I didn't have the strength to do it."

"Can you go get it?"

A shiver of fear runs up Antoine's spine, but he doesn't dare retreat now. When he returns to the terrace, he busily sets up a tape player. While he does, Laura explains:

"It was when Rosa was gone, when she first went to France to prepare things for our move, that I came into possession of these documents. They were given to me by a woman who introduced herself as a journalist and said her name was Dolores. She came one afternoon, riding in Ovid's ramshackle pick-up truck. Ovid lived right near us. A taxi driver, Rosa trusted him completely. Of course, he was one of her informants—his job was to report on the conversations of his passengers. He had come across Dolores as she was climbing up the path one Saturday morning, when the sun was burning hot. Being friendly, he'd stopped. When he learned she was looking for Rosa's house, he was quite happy to make himself useful and brought her right there.

I was standing on the balcony outside my bedroom when I heard the vehicle screech to a stop. While Ovid hit the horn, the woman opened the door and jumped out on her short legs. She was quite tiny, really. I hurried down from the terrace to meet them. I started to stammer, like always, explaining that Rosa wasn't there, that I couldn't invite her in. Without waiting, Ovid pulled the door shut and took off. I quickly realized that Dolores was thrilled that Rosa wasn't there and that she was doing all she could to tell me not to be afraid, that I could trust her. She was a little woman, with a slight yellow cast to her skin—clearly a *métisse*. I remember her delicate features, and the anguish I could glimpse on her face. Her nails and fingers had taken on the color of her eyes—a greenish brown, if truth be told—because she smoked, avidly inhaling cigarette after cigarette. Her straw-colored hair was arranged in a bun, a sort of corkscrew high on her head. She said she was a filmmaker and was preparing a documentary on the "women in steel trousers." That's why she'd made the trip to Haiti from Washington, DC, where she lived. On the other side of the island, in the Dominican Republic, another woman, a certain Josepha Henriquez, enjoyed the same reputation as Rosa; she'd been accused of being involved in the assassination of the *Mariposas*,[1] whose car had been run off the road, down into a ravine, killing all three of them.

Dolores claimed that she wanted to gather more information, but in truth she already knew quite a lot. She asked me if she could visit the secret underground cells. Seeing the panic written on my face, she knew she was asking too much. During a stay in France, she explained, she'd met a group of exiles who'd just been expelled from the country. They'd given her a detailed account of the hell they'd experienced in Duvalier's prisons—they all talked about Rosa.

The tapes in the box are recordings of some of their testimony. If you want, we can listen to one, the first, labeled Janice Brisset. That testimony tells in agonizing detail the nightmarish story of a raid organized by Rosa on a banana field. Apparently, my parents met their deaths during that raid, one of those that the Supreme Leader called "extraordinary expeditions." Long afterwards, I realized why Dolores was so insistent about leaving me her name and address. No doubt she hoped to help me if Rosa were ever put on trial.

Having survived that raid, Janice Brisset, whose testimony we'll hear, was imprisoned. After the son, the famous Baby Doc,

---

1 "Mariposas" (butterflies, in Spanish) is the name given to the three Mirabal sisters—Patria Mercedes, Maria Argentina Minvera, and Antonia Maria Teresa. They opposed the dictator Rafael Leonidas Trujillo, and were assassinated on November 25, 1960.

assumed the throne, she was exiled to France, and was supposed to testify for the film Dolores was making. Antoine, I'll spare you the account of the emotions, the feelings that overcame me several years later, after we'd settled here in France, when I finally found out what was in these documents I'd hidden from Rosa. But now, as you put it so well, the hour has come.

16

Laura presses the button. Janice's voice begins to roll off the spool. Hesitant at first, she slowly grows more confident and, as if in a nightmare, the unbearable scenes she describes emerge, one after the other.

The Testimony of Janice Brisset, recorded in Montreuil, France, 1988.

Félix Bosquet and his wife, Marie-Aimée Lucas, two leaders of our cell, had gone to meet a guy who was supposed to deliver ammunition. Neither of them ever came back. We found them in the morning, tied to a tree, not far from the cottage where we'd sought refuge. They'd been decapitated. Their eyes had been gouged out and their heads, staring at us with empty bloody sockets, placed on their knees. It was Béatrice, Marie-Aimée's sister, who found them. Early in the morning, she was going to a little stream to get water. We heard her howl as if her whole body was just one vast chest erupting in a sob. It was ... how can I say it, it was a soul's last cry, the one released before you lose your mind. Béatrice was with Philippe, the poet, who had the habit of scribbling on anything he could put his hands on. He always had a copy of Verlaine's *Alcools* in the pocket of his smock, as well as a little notepad that was falling apart, in which he had copied poems by Roussan Camille, and that marvelous text by Jacques Roumain, *Bois d'ébène*. Right when the machine-gun fire started popping in the banana field, Philippe shot himself in the temple, and Béatrice, completely shattered, turned and rushed back to our camp, where she collapsed in my arms.

In our cottage, which had two tiny rooms, there was no way out, no way to retreat. Outside, the militia were screaming like madmen. We were terrified. They informed us that we were nothing but ashes and blood, already swept into the thick layer of silence blanketing the country.

Gil wanted to set the cottage on fire. We had gasoline and matches. I refused, as did Gérald, who said he wanted to sink his eyes into the minds of his executioners right as they were about to shoot him. We waited. We only had three rusty rifles left; we'd run out of ammunition for the machine-gun. A contact was supposed to bring us supplies from Florida, but he had disappeared after pocketing all the money we'd struggled to scrape together for him.

They kept us pinned down for five days, with no food and no water. At the end of the third night, Béatrice, who'd been lying prostrate since making it back, started singing a hymn to the Virgin. How could I forget her voice, weak from hunger and thirst: "In heaven, in heaven, in heaven, I'll see her one day." Annoyed by her song, Gérald rushed over and grabbed her by the throat. Béatrice gave a small little yelp and fell, unconscious. Fear, exhaustion, that sensation of being caught in a trap like little mice, had us all out of our minds. At night, along with the chirping of crickets, we could hear Rosa's troops singing: *"Mache pran yo, mache pran yo*—Forward, forward, forward, we'll get them." I'll never get those murderous chants out of my mind. Duvalier and his men had managed to surround this country with an unbroken, never-ending ring of fear. They wanted there to be an assassin hiding behind each man and each woman. Beneath each of our steps, from under every rock, fear should burst forth. So many people that we thought were safe from this decrepitude had joined the ranks of the assassins, donning the paramilitary's blue uniform. Doctors abandoned their patients and hospital posts, lawyers walked out of their offices to join the parade, proudly wearing the blood red scarf. Some innocent souls hoped that behind those dark glasses a glimmer of shame remained, a whiff of dignity. Alas, as time passed, the assassins were emboldened; they distilled their poison, poisoned our consciences.

The soldiers made a game of repeatedly setting fire to the beams holding up the cottage, then putting it out with their hoses. One of the members of our group was a boy named Josué, the son of a protestant pastor who was said to be very close to Duvalier. By the end of the third day, we had a hard time calming down Gérald, who'd decided we'd been betrayed by Josué and that he needed to be tried and judged. How could we know just who was who in this climate of gratuitous accusations and untruthful confessions? People denounced others before anyone could denounce them;

fingers were pointed to deflect those pointed their way. Josué's face twisted into an awful mask that betrayed his fear as he recited psalms while aiming the unloaded machine-gun at the door. Meanwhile, Béatrice, who'd finally come to, got down on her knees and started singing and praying again. She'd always taken herself quite seriously, loved to say that she was born a Marxist. As proof, she claimed to have thrown the rosary from her first communion into the septic tank. In a raspy voice, she recited the *Ave Maria* without missing a syllable in the whole series, and I just sobbed nonstop. On the morning of the last day, Gil, the youngest of the group—he was only sixteen—decided to go out with his hands up, to show we were turning ourselves in. A burst of machine-gun fire welcomed him. They burst through the door, tore the clothes off our backs. With our hands bound behind us, they pulled us along by a rope tied around our necks. They made us parade through the town, as they shouted, "Vive Duvalier, President for Life!" A solid row of people, frozen in place by fear, watched us go by.

Then they took us in old ox-carts pulled behind trucks all the way to the capital, to the presidential palace where Duvalier himself greeted us, along with Rosa Bosquet and a group that included someone named Cambronna and Benjamin Trelas, as well as several other subordinates—the ones whose names I remember were Jean Broiveau, Jean Remon Claude, Norcemer, Angelot Bontemps, Franco Nero, and that really sick animal, a guy named Daisir, who fulfilled his job as a torturer with a bowler hat on his head and a Bible in the pocket of his jacket. Between each torture session, he'd recite psalms.

They spent the next three days and three nights on what they called our trial. Those brutes, with their eyes so white and cold as ice, and Duvalier, who looked like a corpse—Duvalier's skin really was grey! I swear, it was absolutely grey, like ashes. For the first time in my life, I was confronted by a man with grey skin, just like a rat. "You are attacking the nation," he declared, with his cavernous voice, each time the interrogations started up again. "You are attacking me! I am and will always be the nation!" Another of his henchmen, Jaquelin Gracia, forced us to repeat each time he brought the whip down on our backs, "He is and will always be the nation!" When they'd leave us there in the torture room, they'd play a recording of some doctor, they said he was a neurologist trained in the United States, director of the Red Cross in Haiti.

He'd bray this sentence that made our blood run cold: "The blood will flow like never before! The land will burn from north to south, from east to west! There will be no more sunrise, no sunset, just a great fire rising up to the sky. It will be the greatest massacre in our history, a Himalaya of cadavers!"

Besides Rosa Bosquet, there was a cohort of men coming and going along the hallways of the palace where our trial took place. Most looked like venerable family fathers or civil servants; only the obsequiousness evident in their gestures, their servile posture, allowed us to identify them as reptiles. After they'd had their fill of torturing us, they separated the men from the women, then threw us into a narrow cell, a hole packed full of women, each more emaciated than the next. The rough plastered walls bit into bruised skin. Unable to lie down, for lack of space, we stayed sitting, lined up along the wall, each woman's elbows jabbing into her neighbor's ribs like spurs. There are no words to describe the place or its overwhelming stench. Worms wriggled over the naked bodies of the prisoners, who didn't even notice anymore. I spent two endless years there. How is that possible? Why didn't I succumb as so many others did? By what trick of nature did I manage to stay alive? How? ... How? I have no answers. I just know that I became a beast, blind and deaf. When we'd hear the moans of those who were being tortured coming to us from the cellars, any remaining doubts I had—any hope for some sign of the least little bit of the humanity that exists in every man and in every woman—disappeared. All that was left was a sharp pain in my gut, an endless cry that was anything but human. From then on, it didn't matter if I heard the howling of those being tortured in the cellars, or the screeching of the tires as cars dropped off our executioners and took them back home after their shift. Nothing touched me anymore. I was nothing, nothing but that cry. I was banished from myself, had declared my own death. Like all the other women, Béatrice and I were raped by the men—not the other prisoners, they didn't have the strength, but almost all the others, from the highest official to the lowest grunt, abused us. I was no longer aware of my body. It had become—how can I say it?—an envelope, an object that didn't belong to me. Little by little, everything was stripped from me, right down to the courage and the strength to feel, or even hate.

One day I realized that Béatrice had gone completely mad. It was early morning. The previous night had been rhythmed by the whistling of bullets and the cries of the dying. They would often empty the prison like that, to make room for new victims. Trucks had kept coming and going all night, and we had waited, Béatrice and I, for them to come for us. We counted their steps along the hallway, shivering as they came nearer, and as they moved on, we gave sighs that we alone heard. Then came dawn, and with it Béatrice's madness. Crouched down beside me, she kept pinching herself, scratching her body, already covered with scabs and scars. She carefully peeled off strips of her flesh, picked out the worms and stuffed everything into her mouth, chewing slowly and then swallowing, saying that was our only chance, the only way to not disappear. "We'll get out of here, bit by bit," she repeated. "Now that we've understood their little game, we have to put a stop to it. This is the best plan, they won't notice a thing." All these years later, Béatrice is still shut away in a sanatorium, an asylum, somewhere near Toulouse. She doesn't recognize anyone and always wears thick gloves. That's the only way to keep her from devouring herself.

Some time after Béatrice had gone mad, I realized that another being that I rejected with all my strength had taken root within me. That's when I began to call on hatred to save me. Hate drains a lot of energy from us but can also give us strength. Before that, I couldn't muster the force necessary to hate them, it took all I had just to survive. But when I understood that those bastards had filled me with their foul seed, that inside of me, sharing my blood, was a being born of their fornication, I became an intense ball of hatred, living only on dreams of murder.

And while they laughed about it, making the raunchiest jokes about who could be the father of that thing growing inside me, I tried everything I could to tear out of my womb that creature whose tentacles latched onto the walls of my belly, sucking out what little life remained. No one took pity on me. Except for a little corporal who reminded me of a grasshopper. He was the butt of their jokes. Sometimes he brought me fresh water and bits of leftover food he pilfered from the kitchen. The more my belly swelled, the more I hated them. My blood was nothing but bitter, boiling fluid. They had broken us, but somewhere, in some hidden corner of my mind, I held on to the belief that we hold within us the key to escape. I was sure there would be some way for us to get out, that one day, someday, we'd lift up the torch again. I promised myself that I'd make them pay for their crimes! You believe in justice like you believe in God or love. It's a foolish hope. We underestimate so much: how hard-hearted humans can be, their meanness, how cruel life is, and, most of all, our extraordinary ability to forget everything. Even today, I wonder where we found the resources we needed to stay alive in that prison, to continue feeding our hope and cherishing our ideals.

When I opened my eyes in that room with blood-spattered walls that served as the prison's clinic, I found the strength to tell them that I would smash the newborn against the wall if they dared hand it to me. Then I lost consciousness—fell so deeply that they thought I was in a coma. Never in all the rest of the time I spent in detention did I ask what they'd done with the baby. After the birth, the women took care of me as best they could, washing me with urine to help heal my wounds. Some went so far as to save a portion of their daily rations for me. It took me ages to recover. Then, we all just pretended to forget about the child. During my detention, I never once met with a lawyer or a doctor, never got news of my family, who had also suffered threats and horrible mental torture. My grandmother Léa died, my father, too, and one of my aunts, Clémence, as well. After two years, they took us out of the prison, those of us who'd survived, put us on a plane, and expelled us from the country. It wasn't until I arrived in Paris that I learned of all who had died. I had to bury my loved ones, all at once, in this immense mass grave I carry within me.

On the day of our departure, there was a very young man with us at the airport, Richard. The host of a radio show out in the countryside, he'd been thrown into prison. The military had cut out his tongue. He was swimming in the clothes they'd given him. The only thing still visible on his face were the whites of his eyes, sunk back into their sockets. Squeezed close next to each other, holding tight to the rusted metal bench in the main hall of the airport, we looked like a colony of skeletons.

And how can I not talk about Cia? Not talk about her pain, because that's all we knew of her. There in the cell, she was no more than an empty shell. They'd gotten rid of everything, leaving her with nothing but the raw mourning of her own being, an incandescent lament that she hummed nonstop. On the day she'd arrived in prison, Cia's face was just a mass of battered flesh, a coarse mask, its features barely sketched. The skin, split, peeled open, like a rotten fruit tossed away on the ground. Cia looked like the carcass of an animal, the hunted prey of other beasts. None of us thought she'd survive. Her memory had been entirely erased, except for the horrible adventure that brought her to prison, and that had begun with the capricious temperaments of two sisters, twins, both *Fillettes Lalo* in the group known as the Ferocious Gazelles, Rosa Bosquet's favorites. All these years later, I still struggle to understand how anyone could feel threatened by a woman like Cia? Of what crime was she accused? Why did they need to attack her? Cia was one of those beings who doesn't even try to find out if life could be better, if their life could be any different. Never, ever, would Cia have tried to stand up to those who oppressed her. And still, they broke her. Until she was released from prison, all she remembered was that story and her first name—what a sad joke, like her life, reduced to just one syllable. Cia, she said it in one puff between her bare gums, always apologetically because it always came with a spurt of saliva, something she couldn't control. "They pulled them all out," she said, so we'd forgive her for spraying us, as she wiped her lips with the back of her hand. "They'll have to pay for this, won't they?"

The day she arrived, I kept my eyes closed tight. She was crouching on the mat next to me. I … I didn't want to look at her, but I could feel her bare body moving, swaying back and forth, and her otherworldly eyes staring at me, searching, hoping for some answer. As soon as her swollen lips were able to open, Cia started telling the same story, over and over again, like an old scratchy record. She told her one and only memory, a memory of her body given over to brute force. Every day, from the moment she woke up, she told and retold the event that had pitched her into the abyss. She told it like a child recites a lesson they've learned and don't want to forget. Since then, Cia's voice has been grafted onto me, filling all the spaces pain hadn't already taken over. Until she was freed, two years later, Cia was, like the rest of us, never tried, never convicted—and she was expelled to a distant country, without ever knowing who she really was.

The morning of our deportation, at the airport, Cia had no idea where she was or where she was going. Yet, just like an animal that senses something is going to happen, she was agitated, speaking fast and without stopping. I tried to forget she was there, the crackling of her voice. Leaning my head against the wall, I tried to learn how to breathe freely again. After all that time in an overcrowded, narrow cell, so much space around me made me feel drunk and nauseated—and the noise from the crowds made it even worse. Still, Cia's voice, like the purring of a cat, pursued me relentlessly: "I laid out all the rolls of cloth. Oh, if you could have seen their faces, they're not just ordinary whores, those *Fillettes Lalo*! But what had gotten into me to make me wander into that neighborhood of criminals? Between you and me, those folks aren't human, they're animals who died a long time ago, rotten carcasses—those *choches* are just rabid bitches. They ordered me to show them everything, down to the last piece of cloth. Then they told me to get the fuck out, saying my merchandise was just junk, good enough for dressing women from the hills, like me, with big fat toes and dirty feet. I swear on the head of my dead mother that I didn't answer back. I just started rolling up my bundles. And I hadn't eaten a thing since the morning, I'd just dragged my old bones up and down those streets full of potholes and rubbish. What could I have eaten? Rubbish? Oh yes, I should have tried to feed myself with rubbish, because I didn't have a cent in my pocket. For two days, I hadn't sold even a penny's worth of cloth, didn't have so much as a grain of salt to put beneath my tongue. It was three in the afternoon, the time when fancy ladies have a siesta, but me, I didn't know what I was going to eat that night or the next day. I had almost finished packing up. But humiliating me and making me waste my time just wasn't enough for them. Everything was packed up. That's when she walloped me right in the mouth. I was so afraid, even if I was certain I hadn't done anything to make them angry. I was scared stiff, trembling like a leaf. The biggest one, the one with a horse face and fake red hair, jumped on me: blow after blow, with her fists, the butt of her revolver, her boots. I saw death coming for me, and oh, she is not beautiful. I felt like a dirty roach they wanted to smash. But even roaches, really, do you have to be so brutal when you kill them? They refused to believe me, when they were interrogating me up there in the room with blood all over the walls. They asked me questions, like I was a criminal. They hit me to make me answer, and when I answered, they said they didn't believe a single word of my story. Anyway, you know better than I just what they're capable of. A girl as beautiful as you, they'd have to be heartless to treat you like that, right? But one day they'll pay for it, or else we'll know that God on high who sees everything, judges everything, is really blind and deaf. A curse on anyone who believes that the wheel will keep turning in the same direction until the end of time!"

Were it not for the presence of representatives from the Red Cross at the airport, they would have gagged her again. But then, it never did any good to ask Cia to be quiet. She even talked in her sleep, curled up on her mat. She talked to the bedbugs, roaches, and crabs, she took all the formidable beasts that shared our cell as her witnesses and told them her story, exhorting them, at least, to show some mercy. At night, Cia would struggle, fighting to save her life. "Let me go, colonel. Madam *Choche*, let me go!"

17

As one, Laura and Antoine silently agree to put an end to this torture. They don't have the strength to talk about what they've heard. Between them, a profound sadness, and a silence far too heavy. Antoine observes Laura's face. Despite the sadness, he sees great kindness. But he notes something else in her eyes, too, something old, a mysterious veil. Uncomfortable being observed so carefully, Laura gets up and steps out into the garden. Antoine follows her. They walk along, heads bowed, each wondering where to begin.

"I am a house infested with termites," Laura says.

"If you find the strength to fight them, that's half the battle." Antoine's voice grows deeper, gravelly. Laura doesn't reply.

"Tell me a bit about yourself," he asks.

Silence.

"Tell me about your childhood," Antoine tries again.

As if a wall suddenly gave way, Laura lowers her guard.

"My earliest childhood has totally disappeared, swallowed up in the ocean of my memory. All that remains are recollections of Julienne, and that day when Rosa appeared at school to take me to her home. As for that moment when I woke up in her house, under the watchful gaze of that doll with blue eyes and blond hair she'd gotten just for me, I'll never forget that. Right then, I felt myself grow cold and hard. Under the doll's icy stare, I became a monster, more monstrous and stronger than Rosa herself. Just before I turned thirteen, when I met a certain Marie-Louise, I realized that a violent poison had seeped into my veins. From then on, there was another person living inside me.

In the milky light of the coming day, another tale is born, signing a death warrant for the character who had suddenly appeared in Laura the day she crossed paths with Marie-Louise.

It was a night in November, during a wake that Rosa needed to attend. This time, uncharacteristically, she ordered Laura to go with her. They got into the big Jeep. Just like Rosa, the driver is wearing dark glasses, even though night has already fallen. He drives down the bumpy roads through a cloud of dust. Rocks explode like firecrackers beneath the tires of the speeding car. To avoid being run over, people on foot hug tight to fences or throw themselves down into the ditch. The car goes up a steep incline, then down into a little valley, and stops in an immense courtyard where several other similar cars are already parked.

A whole crowd of men and women, all wearing the blue uniform and red scarf, are already there. They hurry to fall into two rows as soon as Rosa appears. Her back straight, kepi on her head, Rosa reviews her troops. Laura doesn't know where to look or what to think. Just who is this woman who claims to be her aunt? No doubt, Rosa must be someone very important for all these people to pay her such respect. Stupefied, Laura stares at those men and women, standing at attention, saluting Rosa so ceremoniously. Some even bow all the way down to the ground as she passes.

Lost in her thoughts, Laura suddenly feels herself pulled backwards. She looks over her shoulder, trips, then turns around and finds herself face to face with a strange character—the first thing she notices is her forehead that glistens in the shadows, and her lips, painted a shocking red. A violent perfume wafts around her. Stunned, Laura examines the clothes the girl is wearing. Her hair is smooth, carefully slicked with brilliantine, and tied in a bun. That makes her forehead look even bigger, like a big greasy fritter. And the lipstick has gotten smeared on her teeth—she looks like a strange sort of clown.

Happy to be noticed, Marie-Louise—that's her name—arches her back and twirls.

"You love my outfit, don't you? I can tell."

Laura doesn't know what to say. Full of condescension, Marie-Louise takes her hand and spins her in a pirouette, then announces her verdict:

"Poor little thing, you're still as flat as an ironing board! Maybe in another two years you'll be ready!"

She continues, "My skirt is a little too long, I think, I ought to take it up. What do you think? What I like is the top, it fits really well, right?" She flashes a smile that shows her red teeth, then pulls up her bra straps to show off her breasts. "Why are you looking at me as if I were a ghost? You look like you've lost your mind. Where did they find you?"

She lifts an authoritative finger and points it at Laura, asking: "First off, who'd you come with?"

"With Rosa."

"Rosa? Rosa Bosquet? You're so lucky!" she snaps, clearly impressed.

She moves closer to Laura, puts an arm around her shoulders. The smell of her armpits mixed with her perfume makes Laura feel queasy. She pulls her head away.

"Why do you say I'm lucky?"

A mean look flashes in Marie-Louise's eyes, as if she envied Laura.

"But ..." Laura tries to explain, "Rosa, she's ... sort of my aunt." She stammers, "That's ... that's what she says ..."

Marie-Louise stares at Laura, who's at a loss for words and hesitates for a moment before adding, sheepishly, "That's all I know."

With a sharp edge to her voice, Marie-Louise retorts, "If that's all you know, then you know absolutely nothing."

Curious, Laura asks her what she knows. Shrewd, Marie-Louise realizes there must be some way to take advantage of her ignorance.

"Come upstairs with me," she orders.

She grabs hold of Laura forcefully and drags her upstairs.

"There's an attic where no one ever sets foot. We won't be bothered there. I'll explain it all to you."

Through a series of loud and garishly lit rooms, Laura follows Marie-Louise, who still has a tight grip on her wrist. Up a narrow spiral staircase to the attic, chock full of all sorts of old things, like all attics are. Grey with dust, two dozen kepis are lined up against a wall. Marie-Louise notices the shock in Laura's eyes and laughs like a fool.

"Your eyes are like a whiting fried in oil that's too hot. It's not the first time you see kepis, is it?" she teases.

Laura stutters something incomprehensible.

"Rosa must have a whole bunch of them, too?"

"I don't know."

"Just what do you know? Your own age, maybe?"

"I'm almost thirteen."

"And you still don't have breasts?"

"No."

"When you're as stupid as you are, you don't need them."

Laura bows her head, embarrassed, but mostly taken aback.

Marie-Louise sits down cross-legged on a dusty matt. With an imperious wave, she motions for Laura to do the same. The girl obeys, as if that was all she'd ever done in life, and sits down facing Marie-Louise.

"Do you know the name and rank of the woman in the coffin?" Marie-Louise asks.

"No."

"Her name is Rita Frédécœur. Her rank was *Vénérable*, that means she was the biggest of all the *reines-choches*, the queen of all the *Fillettes Lalo*. Because she was very old, you didn't see her too much. Now, Rosa's taking her place, she becomes the *Vénérable Reine-Choche*, supreme leader of all the *Fillettes Lalo*! Just imagine, she comes right after the Supreme Leader himself!"

"So, what, really, do *Fillettes Lalo* and the *reines-choches* do?"

"What do they do? Oh, little girl," Marie-Louise coos, adopting a mysterious tone and lowering her voice. "Either you are doing this on purpose, or you really are an idiot. Are you sure you know absolutely nothing?"

She wrinkles her eyebrows and casts a sideways glance at Laura before continuing.

"Their job, first and foremost, is to obey the Supreme Leader, to jump whenever he moves his little finger or waves his baton, and to advise him. But their power goes far beyond that. They are, as my father puts it, the arms, eyes, and feet of the Supreme Leader. The Supreme Leader is the chief of all chiefs, the biggest ever. He does what he wants when he wants, and everything in this country belongs to him, even you and me. If he asks Rosa to send you to his palace this very night, you have to go. If he wants to keep you there for the rest of your life, you can't say no. If he decides somebody has to die, well, they're done for. As for the *reines-choches*, it's the same. Everyone has to obey them. They make sure the wishes of the Supreme Leader are carried out."

"You think it was the Supreme Leader who decided I had to live with Rosa?"

"Who else do you think it could be? His wishes are orders, and you have to learn to anticipate them if you want to get in his good graces. Papa calls that the strategy of thoughtfulness."

"And why would he want me in his palace?"

That is just too much for Marie-Louise; her eyebrows shoot up.

"To do whatever he asks, anything at all … You could scratch his head, suck on his toes, who knows?"

Laura grimaces.

Marie-Louise forces herself to snigger, then leans over and whispers something dirty in Laura's ear. With a haughty sneer she adds:

"We'll never know how many people would give up everything they own just to kiss the Supreme Leader's ass!"

"You're out of your mind!" Laura protests.

That assessment seems to rile up Marie-Louise, who inches even closer to Laura. Their knees touch.

"You must have heard those songs on the radio, the ones everyone is singing to celebrate the great chief's birthday? All the bands in the country had to compose something in his honor, and everyone, from east to west, north to south, has to dance to the tunes."

As she speaks, she points her index finger right in Laura's face.

"That's an idea Rosa and my father came up with," she goes on. "Seems the Supreme Leader was really happy and gave them a big reward. One of the songs goes like this." She starts to hum and sway: "*'Roule, roule papa, pèp ou anfòm dèyè w. 22 mai nou t ap tann pou n antere lenmi.* Go on, go on Papa, your people are behind you. We're waiting for May 22 to bury the enemy.' My father almost died laughing as he tried to show us how, at a party in honor of the regional leader, the peasants from Rivière Goyave danced to a waltz composed by the orchestra Les Tigres du Printemps. Besides being as clumsy as oxen, those folks never wear shoes and had never heard an instrument other than a drum. Seems it was quite a treat to watch them waltz."

"Were they really forced to?"

"Of course! And when they kicked up a fuss, well, then the *Fillettes Lalo* went into action."

"How?"

"They dragged those who didn't want to dance to the middle of the dance floor and cut off their toes!"

Laura refuses to believe all the nonsense spewed out by Marie-Louise, but she still cries out in terror and almost topples over on her back. Marie-Louise catches her and starts in on a lecture.

"You have to learn to open your eyes, little girl! And to be less of a softie, too. Your dear Aunt Rosa, how is she when she comes home after work at night? You've never seen her?"

"No."

"Well, try and catch a glimpse one night when she gets back. Her work isn't easy, you know. Every day, with my father, she has to preside over the tribunal. Sometimes, it's just them, sometimes the Supreme Leader is there, too. A job like that, it's not for little dolls, let me tell you. As for me, my father says I'm going to have an amazing career. He says I'll be a *reine-choche*, respected just like Rosa."

Laura wishes she had something to share, to seem less stupid, but can't come up with anything interesting enough. She vaguely recalls having seen Rosa when she got back one night, her kepi on backwards, her shirt hanging down ... And suddenly, like a child who just starts reciting anything at all in the middle of an oral exam, she hears herself saying, "I have seen her, her ... her clothes all in a mess one night. She was threatening someone and shouting, 'Out with it!' But then I realized she was just talking to herself ..."

"That's all you've got?" Marie-Louise is quick to snigger, more entertained than terrified.

"Yes, that's all."

"When I was twelve, I knew a lot more than you do."

"And how old are you?" Laura stammers.

"Fifteen. But I look eighteen, right?" she says, puffing out her chest.

Laura looks hard at Marie-Louise's face. She notices her almond-shaped eyes, hardened by that desire for domination and power she makes no effort to hide. They're a strange color, a brown that dulls into black, but her eyelids, weighed down by a layer of blue, make them look heavy and crass. The curve of her eyebrows, plucked too high, undermines the delicacy of her features. Her face is just a horrible mask. Marie-Louise's eyes flash and Laura just stares, as a wave of panic floods over her. Any little thing, Laura tells herself, and she'll reduce me to ashes. Instinctively, she recoils. But the other leans in closer, brushing her hand against her chest.

She asks if anyone has felt her up and before Laura can even get a word out, she pounces, grabbing her head and trying to shove her tongue into her mouth. Terrified, Laura pushes her away as hard as she can, driving her elbows into the girl's ribs. Marie-Louise nimbly grabs one of her own breasts, pops it out of her top, and presses it against Laura's mouth. Her lips clenched, Laura chokes, hears her own heart pounding. She lets her know she could bite. Marie-Louise slightly relaxes her grip, but moaning as if she's about to be sick, she begs:

"Suck, suck … You big idiot, just suck, c'mon!"

Laura struggles for all she's worth. In a burst of anger, Marie-Louise lets her go.

"You're such an idiot!" Marie-Louise rages, not knowing what to do given Laura's unexpected reaction, her body as stiff as a pole and such a look of disgust on her face. Suddenly, she explodes:

"You're such a ninny! Like a basket of parsley, you're good for nothing. It's lucky that you're with Rosa, otherwise, you'd have a hell of a time surviving in this country, little girl. Soon Rosa will teach you to obey, you'll see!"

She gives a violent shove and Laura falls on her back. She immediately grabs hold of her, pulls her up and pokes a threatening finger in her face:

"If you're really working for Rosa, you need to smarten up; otherwise, all bets are off. Is she really your aunt?"

Laura shrugs. Marie-Louise imitates her, but as she readjusts her clothes, she gets another idea. Lying down on her back, she stretches out her legs, then pulls them up and slips a finger into a slit, pink, almost mauve. Laura's ears are filled with her gasps and start to burn.

"Oh, it's so good, you can't believe it! Do you want to try? Here, look …"

Marie-Louise twists and turns like a worm, crossing and uncrossing her legs, huffing and squirming frantically.

"If we do it together, it's a hundred times better, I swear! I promise, you've never tasted anything sweeter."

Determined, she swiftly sits up and grabs hold of Laura's hand, trying with all her might to slip it between her legs. Laura shouts, threatens again to bite her. Marie-Louise lets go. Laura retreats into a corner. Pulled tightly into a ball, her shoulders clenched, her back stiff as a rod, she doesn't know if what she feels is disgust, curiosity, or fear. She's hot, burning up, and starts to think of Julienne, who spends so much time correcting her posture, making her sit with her thighs held tightly together, telling her that the wind coming in through the wide-open windows can blow all sorts of dirty things up there and turn us, little by little, into sewers. Just another of Julienne's crazy stories. How can I ever tell her, when I see her again, that right there, just a few centimeters in front of me, Marie-Louise was letting herself go, with the windows wide open, loudly moaning with pleasure.

Voices filter up from below. Marie-Louise doesn't care. Like a marionette with broken strings, her limbs flail about—you'd swear she was having some sort of epileptic seizure. Laura thinks of how to get out of there. To reach the door, she'd have to step over Marie-Louise, who can just quickly grab her legs. She jumps when a wild groan escapes from Marie-Louise's throat—she's panting, faster and faster. Laura pulls back against the wall. Marie-Louise lowers her legs, twists from side to side. Silence. Laura thinks she's fainted. After a moment, the girl yawns, sits up with a snort and seems surprised to see Laura's still there. Her face all red, she stands up and snaps:

"Oh, I'm so hot! It's just too hot in here."

Then, as if nothing at all had happened, she goes back to their conversation.

"You may be just a stupid little fool, I'm still going to give you some advice. Rosa's the most powerful woman in the country, and power, that's all that counts. You have to learn to obey her, do everything she wants, you understand—everything, absolutely everything she asks. You'll be rewarded by becoming one of the most feared women in the country, too. No worries for your future! Do you understand?" she insists, grabbing Laura by the forearm. "You, my little dearie, you have it all on a silver platter.

Marie-Louise dusts off her clothes, smooths her hair and, with a look of pity in her eyes, starts patting Laura's arms and butt, shaking her head all the while.

"You have to eat more. You're too skinny. Nothing but bones!"

Laura feels awkward, like she's shrinking beneath Marie-Louise's self-assurance. To hide her embarrassment, she asks the girl if her father is one of Rosa's men.

"What a question! You really mean you've never heard of Franco Nero? You've never seen him at Rosa's? Impossible!"

"But it's true!"

Another slew of curses. Her mouth twists in indignation.

"You're just a big nuthin', that's plain to see. Franco Nero, he's Rosa's right-hand man, and he's my father," she says proudly. "He's known everywhere in the country. In other words, you're the only person who doesn't know who he is. I just have to say his name at school and everyone gets the hell outta my way. My brother, he carries a pistol and knows how to use it, too. In class, the first thing he does is set it on top of his desk. The teachers just fall into line. Anyone who dares to give him bad grades had better watch out. Soon he'll get his law degree without ever stepping foot in law school!"

"But how can that be?" Laura protests.

"Because he is Franco Nero's son, that's all! It's the same thing for the dauphin; otherwise what use is power, huh, you little nuthin'? You have to see how some students just crawl at his feet."

"At whose feet?"

"My brother's! Are you ever gonna wake up? They all want to get invited to our house, and most of all, to be seen in his big Jeep. As for the girls, what wouldn't they do to catch his eye? You can't even imagine the compliments and the curtseys, just because he's best friends with the dauphin. You know who I'm talking about, don't you?"

Marie-Louise wrinkles her brow.

"Between you and me, I don't think he's that cute," she adds in a whisper. "He's fat like a piglet, am I right?"

"I've never seen him."

"You're lying!"

"It's the truth!"

"Me, I've run into him a few times. Not my type. Besides, he's only interested in cars—I'm sure he sleeps with them!"

Clapping one hand over her mouth, she laughs as if what she just said was really funny.

"Do you have a big Jeep like your brother?"

"Not yet, but it won't be long. My father says I have to earn that car with the sweat of my brows. I won't be one of those weak, little women who drive around in fancy cars because they're sleeping with some guy. But that's what'll happen to you if you don't stop being so stupid!"

They go down from the attic. At the foot of the stairs, Marie-Louise whispers in her ear:

"My father says that I'll be an exceptional *Fillette Lalo* because I never let myself get soft. That's why he takes me everywhere with him, even if I'm only fifteen. At sixteen, I can start training. They'll give me a blue uniform and a beautiful kepi and I'll do my hair just like Rosa."

"The wheel of life and death turns and turns, the wheel of life and death, in its immutable course, deprives us today of our dearly beloved Rita Frédécœur. Oh, spirits and sacred divinities, in your benevolence, receive our all-powerful leader with the honors she deserves." Back in the courtyard, Marie-Louise and Laura are greeted by those words pronounced by a pot-bellied man who leans on a trestle in front of the coffin. Many women are there. Marie-Louise greets some of them as they pass, and explains to Laura that they've come from the four corners of the country to pay their respects. Everyone is wearing dark glasses, but Laura recognizes Rosa thanks to her hair, which you can see, rolled in smooth curls beneath the kepi she has put on to protect her hairdo. One after the other, the men and women who want to speak step up to the trestle and recite a prayer or a panegyric—a litany of praise in honor of the *reine-choche*, Rita Frédécœur.

The minutes pass by slowly, the monotones of the flatterers punctuated by coughs and the awful sound of people clearing their throats. Marie-Louise just can't keep still. She drags Laura to the back of the courtyard. Laura wonders what she's going to come up with this time. Under a palm tree, a wooden bench. Marie-Louise sinks down onto it.

"I've had enough of all their rambling, sit down there," she says, placing a hand on Laura's leg. "No one will bother us. Soon they'll move on to the supreme sacrifice, and I don't feel like taking part. Have you already taken part in a supreme sacrifice?"

"No."

Laura starts to tremble just at the thought of what it could be. Marie-Louise whispers,

"I know this house like the back of my hand. There's even a prison in the basement. I went there and saw bones. I took them."

Laura is convinced that Marie-Louise is trying to frighten her.

Oblivious to the effect of her words, Marie-Louise confides that she has a huge collection of bones.

"Do you want to see the prison?"

"Not now."

Frozen with fear, Laura's voice is no more than a thin string.

"I know everything there is here because I spent two years with Rita."

"Doing what?"

"Getting trained. Don't ask me to explain. You'll find out when the time comes. Rosa will teach you everything."

Suddenly out of patience, she stands up and shouts furiously:

"Do you hear them, those hypocrites! My father calls them the Pharisees, children of Judas, sons of Cain. Listen to them, so full of themselves: Rita this, Rita that, a well of kindness, a mama with a heart as big as Heaven. Rita, my ass, my turds, and my balls!"

She makes that vulgar sound with her lips, like spurting water, giving full vent to her unparalleled disdain, then rages on:

"They're all lying. Not a single one of them loved her. Because she wasn't one to give gifts, no Rita wasn't, and I often saw her kicking their ass. During training sessions, she'd make them slog through shit and eat it, I swear. 'That's the job,' she always told me. 'A woman has to be three times as hard and authoritarian,' she'd say, 'that's what you need to learn.' Because they think women lack courage, that they can't command. The only way to show them our strength is to be a thousand times tougher than all of them. You know, that's why the Supreme Leader prefers to name women to lead the National Security Volunteers. We don't let anything slip by. Result: absolute efficiency! Mandate: give no pity, take no quarter!"

"But what is the supreme sacrifice?"

Laura wants to know, but immediately regrets saying anything, because her voice trembles so.

"Wait!" Marie-Louise commands. "I'm not done! The job of a *Fillette Lalo* requires you to be alert. But you, if you were trying to show off how stupid you are, you couldn't do any better!"

Hand on her hip, she adopts a spiteful tone.

"Really, I am getting tired of you! If you knew all the risks that come with this job! First, no one really loves you, even if they say the opposite and lick your boots."

"Why?"

"Why? Why? Is that stupid word the only one in your mouth? What you need to know is that people are jealous. Period! They all are: of what you have, of your money, your power, and most of all, your connections to the Supreme Leader. You'll have to study the Supreme Leader's Grey Book and the Catechism of the Revolution. There's a chapter, "The Draw of Power." There you learn how to detect flatterers, boot-lickers, all those my father calls the race of ass-offerers."

Marie-Louise begins to snigger silently as she mimics with many pirouettes and bows what ass-offerers do. Seeing Laura's confusion, she realizes she'll have to follow her eloquent demonstration with a detailed explanation.

"You still don't understand? Everything in life has to be earned. Some people only get there by spending all their time offering up their ass. Do you understand?"

"But what are the risks you have to take in this job?"

"Oh no!" Marie-Louise guffaws. "This is a waste of my time."

She falls silent for a moment, then starts whispering.

"Do you know, I already took part in an expedition?"

"An expedition? To where?"

"Uh, well ... here," she says, starting to get excited again.

"In this town?"

"No, in a place called Cazale."

"During summer vacation?"

"No. When there's an expedition, I don't go to school."

"Really?"

"My father insists training is just as important as what they teach in class, and he's right."

Laura gives up trying to understand. Marie-Louise continues with a look of callous madness in her eyes.

"The expedition lasted several days. We cleaned out a hideout of *Camoquins*."

She pauses and waits for a reaction from Laura, who just can't keep herself from asking what *Camoquins* are.

"Bandits! They're very dangerous. You're better off fighting *lougawou* or all the demons in hell. My father says they're parasites come from abroad to destroy everything good in this country. And they call that a revolution! Like all parasites, they must be exterminated. For them, all people must be equal. And they'll do anything to reach their goal. You have to avoid them like the plague, you understand. You have to hunt them, squash them, denounce them to the Supreme Leader. The ones we cleaned out were ready to set the whole country on fire, bleed it dry, take our houses and everything we own and give it all to those who don't have any. My father said he was going to pulverize them like cockroaches, like giant palmetto bugs. I promise you, we didn't go easy on them!

"What did you do?"

"All turned into the past tense!"

"How?"

Laura's heart beats wildly when, in the shadows, she glimpses a sinister glow in Marie-Louise's eyes, the look of an animal about to pounce.

"Do I have to spell it out for you? Well, we left them to starve, locked up in their trap, then we threw bottles filled with gasoline and set fire to the house they were hiding in. Grilled like big fat roaches! Then, to wrap it up, we exterminated all the peasants who'd given them shelter and food!"

"Is that true?"

"The speeches are over. Now on to the sacrifice," Marie-Louise announces, and then adds, "When you're a *reine-choche*, you belong body and soul to the Supreme Leader. That's why, when you die, they have to take out your heart, your liver, your kidneys, and offer them to him."

"Are you sure?"

Laura's teeth are chattering. Marie-Louise notices and puts her arm around her neck.

"All of this frightens you, huh, my little nuthin'? Don't you worry, you'll get used to it soon."

"You still didn't answer!" Laura insists, her voice shaky. "Are you telling the truth?"

"As true as you're a first-class idiot and my name is Marie-Louise Nero, future *reine-choche*," she chuckles.

Struggling to swallow her saliva, Laura still can't stop herself from asking,

"Why do you have to do that?"

"Why?"

Marie-Louise pauses, thinks for a moment, then quickly responds,

"It's part of the tests they make the recruits go through. At one moment or another, each recruit must take part in a supreme sacrifice ceremony. The Supreme Leader, master of all goods and all lives, keeps these organs in a secret room, organized in little boxes, and, believe me, it's a great honor for a volunteer to end his career in one of those little boxes. From the men, they also take their dangly thing, little or big," she adds.

Leaning in close to Laura's ear, she murmurs,

"Rita said that once they're dead, that pretentious thing that makes them lose their head and often turns women into idiots is no better than an earthworm!"

Impelled by some evil idea, Marie-Louise grabs Laura by the arm and drags her to the center of the courtyard, where the ceremony is taking place. In a panic, Laura resists.

"Come!" Marie-Louise commands, her eyes shining bright with excitement.

Laura is trembling from head to toe, gasping, wondering how she'll get out of there.

"Don't be an idiot, come!"

Marie-Louise enjoys the terror she sees in Laura's eyes. She gives one of her sardonic laughs while Laura, still struggling, is as silent as a dead fish. Marie-Louise thinks she needs to come up with a better plan, but right then Laura sees a man holding what looks like a cutlass and screams for all she's worth. Her head spins and she faints. Marie-Louise has seen worse, so she doesn't lose her cool. She runs off to get water and sprinkles it on Laura's face.

When Laura opens her eyes, she's lying on a bed inside the house. Rosa is standing in front of her.

"We're going home!" she commands.

18

Rosa never saw Marie-Louise again. Yet, she never really left her. Her screechy voice, like a shrike's, her irritating, unhealthy self-confidence, the smell of her breasts, that perfume she doused herself with, all those memories left Laura uncomfortable. Since that memorable night, she felt she'd lost some part of herself, that another being had slipped inside her.

Back at the house, later that night, Laura observes Rosa carefully. Watches her take off her boots and her heavy belt. For the first time, Laura notices the bulge in her pants pocket, revealing the presence of a pistol. That's when she realizes that Rosa is never without it, becomes aware of how important it is to her. Rosa asks her if she's sleepy; Laura shakes her head no. Rosa offers some fruit juice and, despite Laura's clear protestations, she calls for Léonie, one of the servants, waking her up at that ungodly hour—it was three a.m.—to make grenadine juice. With an unusual show of kindness, Rosa invites Laura to join her in the formal living room. It's an austere room, the only one in the house that Laura actually likes. The antique furniture in burnished mahogany and the huge wicker armchairs remind her of her grandmother Belle's living room. The peaceful atmosphere invites you to relax, yet Laura never goes there because it's where Rosa retreats, whenever she can.

Rosa settles down in a wingback chair and asks how she liked Nero's daughter Marie-Louise's company. Instead of replying, Laura stares at the grandfather clock that just struck three. Rosa praises Marie-Louise's seriousness, her docility, and her intelligence.

"Nero puts all his trust in her," she explains. "Even at her age, she clearly has a good head on her shoulders. Soon you'll be thirteen, you should follow her example."

Laura keeps silent. A worried look flashes across Rosa's face. She gets up, grabs her bag, pulls out a comb and starts re-braiding her hair. Her nimble fingers fly quickly over her locks, and her painted fingernails make Laura think of bright little beetles. After a moment, she holds the comb out to Laura and asks her in a honied voice:

"Come, my pretty, my arms are tired. Come help me."

Without really thinking, Laura says no. Her harsh tone makes Rosa jump. She wasn't expecting that, and tries to hide her disappointment by pasting a sad look on her face and murmuring,

"I thought you'd like to."

She scowls and glares at Laura. Frozen in place, Laura feels a vague wave of fear welling up in her, which she instinctively feels she should hide. After a moment, she pretends to be falling asleep. She shuts her eyes but then quickly opens them again, preferring to return Rosa's gaze.

That night, with the ingenuity of an orchestra conductor, Rosa arranges a score for two musicians. She starts talking, making large circles with her arms as she does her hair, sending waves of her perfume wafting through the room. With each braid, she weaves her life together with Laura's, forever: Laura and she, joined at the hip, inseparable, until death do them part.

"We'll do this, we'll do that ..."

She suggests a trip to Italy: she's always dreamed of seeing Rome, Capri, and especially Venice, floating along on a gondola. But while Rosa seeks to overwhelm her with a wave of words, something fierce begins to grow deep inside Laura, a pitiless disdain born of the nausea rising up within her, as powerful as a floodtide.

Slunk back in her seat, across from Rosa, Laura no longer feels like herself. In that instant, she is transformed by everything she is taking in, by this strange scene where she is at once actress and spectator. The intense clouds of Rosa's expensive perfumes will never manage to cover up the stench of rot that floats around her, filling this huge house where Laura never ought to have set foot. Those violent scents have seeped into her, she realizes in a flash of lucidity, as if she'd suddenly aged a thousand years.

Rosa has had too much to drink. Her tongue is thick and pasty. Laura wonders how anyone can drink so much alcohol and not die. She senses that being intoxicated is like a façade for Rosa, that alcohol is a sort of crutch, just as it is for all the men and women who serve under Rosa's command. That flash of insight doesn't spare her from the fear that chills her to the bone as she listens to Rosa talk about the Supreme Leader, a visionary, a man of unequaled courage. Does Rosa not see the difference between cowardice, savagery, and valor?

After another hour, during which she talked nonstop, Rosa declares that it's time for bed. Without waiting to be asked twice, Laura stands up. That's when Rosa, with a quick, awkward bound, jumps up and grabs her around the waist, rubbing her skin against Laura's cheek. Laura shudders in horror. Rosa covers her neck and hair with audible kisses, repeating that Laura will never know how much she loves her. At first, Laura thinks it's some sort of joke, tells herself that Rosa really did drink too much, but then she stiffens and grows threatening herself. First, that Marie-Louise, and now Rosa. Like a porcupine, Laura's quills bristle, and she destroys any and all pathways that might lead Rosa to her. Her heart is pounding loudly when Rosa, with her authoritarian grip, pulls her tight to her hip and, on unsteady feet, drags her toward the stairs leading up to the bedrooms. At the foot of the stairs, Laura gathers up all the courage her frail body contains and manages to break free. Rosa loses her balance, stumbles, and grabs hold of the banister. Laura races up the stairs. Rosa's words, interspersed with drunken sobs, haunt her long after.

"Laura, come back, you know how I love you ... I'm all you have ... I love you, Laura!"

At dawn, Julienne found Rosa asleep on the carpet in front of her bedroom door.

If, thanks to Julienne, Laura learned how to move through despair like you wade through flood waters without being carried away, those assaults by Marie-Louise and Rosa allowed her to make hatred her own. That night of the funeral, her eyes were opened once and for all to the violence of the world that lay at her doorstep since she'd arrived in Rosa's home. But if hatred is mainly suffering, it is also chaos. Laura hated Rosa without fully acknowledging it. She abhorred Rosa's monstrous shrewdness, so evident when she had adopted her, made her the heir to her curse. Just like Nero possessed Marie-Louise, Rosa possessed her. She dragged her off along the paths laid out by the Supreme Leader, even though the rebellious spirit of Laura's seven-year-old self never abandoned her, still spurred her on to resistance. Rosa's advances only exacerbated the chaos inside Laura. After that night, she began calling her

Aunt Rosa. But mostly she stayed walled up in her fierce silence. During the long conversations Rosa initiated, conversations meant, so she claimed, to reveal certain truths to her, Laura noted the weak points in Rosa's justifications, how she failed to prove the truths she put forward. Rosa was stumbling along, making things up, lying, losing patience. Her voice quivered with indignation as she railed against the disorder caused by the *Camoquins.*

Several weeks later, Julienne was carried away after a brief illness. Another trial for Laura. A heavy cloud of melancholy surrounded her from then on, and she wondered just what role Rosa had played in that premature death. What if, she wondered, Julienne had gotten in the way, what if she knew too much about her strange boss?

One of Rosa's relatives took charge of running the big household. That surly woman had one shoulder that stuck up higher than the other and answered to the strange name of *Choutte*. She watched over the house like a vulture watches its prey, and barely spoke, for which Laura was grateful. Laura learned to pick up on and decipher with astounding precision all the little noises in the house, the slightest of murmurs wafting up from below. In the silence of her bedroom, she wondered, looked for answers, wanted to figure everything out: her parents' disappearance, as well as Julienne's, all about the Supreme Leader and the others, so she could understand against whom, against what to direct the flood of hatred welling up in her.

The Thursday evening dinners that Rosa organized for her troop of volunteers provided a wealth of information. Laura would listen to the vulgar cries of the harpies coming up from the ground floor, the heated exchanges and the dirty jokes, which were the specialty of a certain Sanette Myrbal, who smoked long, slender cigars with a cigarette-holder. The others kept telling her to be quiet, but she paid no mind.

When the meal was over, Rosa would ask those who belonged to the gang she called her "Ferocious Gazelles" to stick around. Today, Laura couldn't recognize their faces, but she still remembered their names: Lysiane, who was as big as a mare and hid, night and day, beneath broad-brimmed straw hats, which made her look like a giant mushroom; May, who seemed to have escaped from a shipwreck—with her sleepy eyes, she looked like a lost sheep. People said she was a cousin of Rosa's from the countryside, signed up as a volunteer despite herself to pay off an old family debt. Insignificant faces, hardened or blank, with interchangeable names: Sony Xock and Tisimone, or Marie-Denise and Nicole—two sisters decked out in wigs of blond or red hair that hung down to their butts, and who always wore, even in the crushing heat, shiny red leather boots that came up to their knees. These gazelles, who always seemed to be dressed for a masked ball, were known for blocking traffic along the main thoroughfares so they could fight like dogs in heat. They were the sort who'd call their seamstresses in the middle of the night to demand alterations, or wake up their maids to have them draw a bath or just flush the toilet. The most ferocious among them, certainly because she was big and imposing, was Lysiane, no question. She always arrived flanked by a pair of twins, Marcelle and Armelle, and two others, named Elsie and Carmen. As soon as the car was parked, Lysiane would neigh, "The Graces are here, with their flowing skirts, open the gate!" Then she'd burst out laughing, a raunchy laugh—and she had every reason to, Lysiane did, because along with a certain Gladys Christoff, whose palace of horrors stood right across from the barracks, she held the coveted position of treasurer of the terror, entrusted by the Supreme Leader with paying the military's wages. Because Gladys also managed the take from their regular thefts at the Tobacco Authority, she was, along with Rita, Lysiane, and Armelle, one of the architects of the regime. Leaving aside their greed and their cruelty, these women saw themselves as the most important people in the country, especially since they were welcomed in all the right places. No, they weren't thieves, much less criminals who terrorized the areas they controlled, leaving death in their wake.

On Thursdays, each of them was expected to report on the activities in their sector. Once the envelopes were distributed, they were given their marching orders: desirable houses to be seized, raids organized to confiscate goods at some market, accusations to submit to the Supreme Leader, lists of students and applicants for the university to go over with a fine-toothed comb. Memorable tussles would break out when they needed to plan celebrations: the Supreme Leader's birthday in April, the victory over the destabilizers of the Supreme Endeavor in May, Volunteers' Day in July, when fearsome gangs from each of the provinces gathered in the capital, and then in September, the anniversary of the start of the Supreme Leader's reign.

In the years before they left the country, did Rosa have an inkling of the upheaval to come? She worked to tighten up the structure of her troops, whose appetites grew more terrifying each day. There were no more limits on their exactions, no one was safe from their evil deeds. Was Rosa simply too preoccupied to try and assault Laura again? The fact is that Laura saw her only rarely, but she no longer had any doubts about the fate Rosa reserved for her.

Laura pauses, then shudders again and again. Her eyes catch Antoine's. She looks away.

19

Silence can be quite eloquent, Laura realizes. She is hesitant to talk about her life in France with Rosa and feels cornered when Antoine says:

"How can we make sense of our equivocation, our good and bad decisions?"

Beneath Antoine's neutral tone, she thinks she hears a hint of a reproach, and her heart races.

"Do you mean my decision to stay with Rosa once I arrived in France?"

Laura lowers her voice, as if to murmur a secret.

"It's true, it's true," she sighs, wringing her hands. "I had such doubts about my ability to stand on my own two feet. How many times did I pack my bags only to unpack them the next day? How many times?" she continues. "You can't understand. There were times when I was losing my mind, completely adrift, forgetting even my own name. I'd stay shut up inside for days and days, without talking or seeing anyone. I went through hell, Antoine. Sometimes I just threw things in my bags ... as fast as I could. It made me feel free, like I was drunk. But once I saw them at my feet, all locked and ready, an overwhelming fear would take hold of me, and I'd empty them out just as fast. You can't know how awful that is. I hated myself, kept beating myself down, telling myself I'd been too eager to drink the Kool-Aid of hypocrisy and lies. Rosa used to repeat this awful phrase—from the catechism of the Duvalierist revolution, she said—I couldn't get it out of my head: 'There are in each of us two very distinct people. One must learn to live with them both.' On the one hand, the unthinkable urges to just let her die and, on the other, the recurring urges to put an end to her life. One day, I came armed with a metal rod I picked up at the hardware store in the village. I wanted, I wanted to pierce her body and enjoy watching her deflate like a balloon. Believe me, I grabbed the handle of the door to her room a hundred times before deciding to take the tool back to the store the next day."

Laura falls silent for a moment. Antoine thinks she's reached the end of her rope, but then she starts up again.

"When I got here, I thought I'd made the logical decision: I'd wait for Rosa to die, since I lacked the courage to kill her myself. Simply wait. Afterwards, I told myself, I'd pick up my life where it had left off. It's true … I wanted to convince myself that one day my life would start up again."

Suddenly she begins to stutter. Unsure of what to do, Antoine tries to move the conversation in another direction.

"You never met anyone with whom you could have built a future, Laura?"

She lifts her head. Antoine sees her eyes are red.

"To think of building a future, as you say, you have to believe you're alive."

Her eyes light up for a moment as she remembers a certain Simonaud, the son of one of Rosa's lieutenants, who seemed head over heels in love with her. She had lost track of him when she'd left for France.

"He was a big lumbering oaf, moved more slowly than a sloth on a branch. He didn't really do anything, and his only real close relationship was with drugs. I'll never find the words to describe how his father always punished him for any little thing. Simonaud Senior seemed possessed by a demon—you'd have thought he'd learned his art in a school run by colonial slavers. Commander of the Volunteers from the town of Cayes-Jacmel, he had no rivals when it came to inventing the most odious of crimes—and that made him the equal of Rosa, Nero, Daisir, Ti Boulé, Gros Féfé, Ti Cabiche, Maîtrelois, Boss Pent, and other pillars of the Duvalier dictatorship. They say he liked to stuff his prisoners in the trunk of his car, trussed up like crabs, then drive to the top of a cliff and throw them in the sea. Simonaud Junior held a silent grudge against this monster, his creator, but it was too late. He was just a shred of a man. Like me, he struggled with his own contradictions. Our brief friendship grew out of compassion. Was it better to grow up without a father or to have a father who was a fearsome beast? I'm sure that by now he's found refuge in Boca Raton, Miami, or Santo Domingo, in one of the haunts of the Duvalierist animals. But ... to get back to when we moved here, Rosa and I ..."

Out of breath, Laura stops.

"You must be tired. Better to let this be for the moment," Antoine suggests. But Laura insists on continuing with the story of what happened before she and Rosa left for France, as if talking about it would help her sort through her overloaded memory.

"Our departure for France is connected to the passing of the Supreme Leader. I was in my second year of an internship with the nuns to become a teacher. The day the news broke, they gathered us all in the chapel for hours, reciting Ave Marias for the peace of the soul of the Father of the Nation. During recess, we walked around in little groups, quietly talking about his disappearance and the changes it would bring. The day of the funeral, heaven blessed me with a high fever and vomiting. I was grateful, because Rosa had planned for me to read a text during the ceremony. The children all had to line up under the hot sun to bow down before the coffin."

"What good luck! Even today I'm sure you give thanks to heaven for sparing you that chore," Antoine quips, trying to make a joke.

"A real stroke of luck, in fact," Laura admits. "With the Supreme Leader's disappearance, rifts began to grow within the troops. Rosa no longer had the same authority over her men. They'd put the reins of power into the hands of the son of the supreme mobster, but they said he was nothing but a puffed-up fool, a simpleton they nicknamed Baby Doc. His speeches seemed less obscure than his father's, and they brought in young technocrats, more modern, but the same political intrigue and bloody purges continued. Everyone was elbowing each other to curry favor with the great galoot. Rosa felt slighted. Her knowledge, her experience meant nothing anymore. The team of fearsome young crooks surrounding the new leader quickly proved just as voracious as their predecessors. Because they thought they were more talented, better educated, with dandified manners, those daddy's boys—some of whom had studied in the United States or in Europe—saw themselves as the aristocrats of the regime. Baby Doc founded a new group to replace Rosa's volunteers. They called themselves the Leopards, and traded the uniforms of rough cloth for fine suits bought from a French couturier. Even the young president's son, a kid just six years old, was dressed up for celebrations in a little blue suit with a red silk scarf, *made in France.*

Just like Rosa's men, these new recruits drove around on the country's potholed roads in the most luxurious cars, killing, pillaging, holding the population hostage. They'd been swimming in crime since they were born and would have finished off Rosa Bosquet in just one bite. After several years of struggles, with dirty tricks coming left and right, she made the wise choice to bow out. She told me about her plans just the day before she was to fly here to get things ready for the move. What could I do, where could I go? I even wondered why it mattered so much to her to take me along. Her plans had failed, she could have just gotten rid of me, left me in a cell. I was of no use to her anymore."

"What do you think she had in mind?"

"One day I asked her that very question, straight out. I told her that things could have taken a very different turn for me, without the death of the Supreme Leader."

"What did she say?" Antoine asks.

"Nothing. Her face just fell, and she looked scared. 'This country will drive us crazy. We have to leave!' was all she said. Her health had started to deteriorate, the lack of power was dragging her down, made her smaller. With no real family, no children, all she had left were the shreds of her power, and her money. Me, I belonged to her and she wasn't going to let me go. All I felt when she told me about her plans was a sharp pain in my heart. I thought about my parents, who'd disappeared. By leaving, I was abandoning them in turn."

Her voice cracks. Big tears roll down her face. Antoine just sits and waits, thanking the heavens that, from then on, he'll no longer be alone on his quest.

"A year after we moved here, Rosa was already very sick. Her sugar levels and blood pressure were out of control, multiple repeated infections, glaucoma and cataracts, arthritis, you get it ... the list is impressive, even without talking about her bulimia, which is just another form of suicide. When she was still walking, she literally lived in the refrigerator. Right out of the container, she just kept stuffing herself, swallowing down everything she could get her hands on. In the course of one evening, I saw her devour a big tray of frozen lasagna, an entire chicken, some dried out fried rice with vegetables, a raw cabbage, a liter of ice cream. One night, she was making so much noise that I heard her in my room, all the way on the other side of the house. Alarmed, I came running.

She was pacing from her room to the terrace, opening all the doors and windows, then she lay down in bed, threw off the sheets. A minute later, she was up again, naked, her hair all over the place, looking like she was possessed. Her limbs were thrashing, her hair was plastered to her temples, violent spasms ran up and down her body. I saw her arch her back against the bed frame and howl, as if beset by demons. As for me, I remained just as she had made me: of marble and granite. I went back and shut myself up in my room.

"Do you think her crimes ever haunt her?" Antoine interrupts, angrily.

Laura catches a note of desperation in Antoine's question. His voice is at a fever pitch. Forgetting Laura's presence for a moment, he starts to murmur. Laura can barely distinguish the two names he repeats, that meld into one: Gala, Mona, Gala, Magala. Antoine's hands clench, his fingers squeezed into tight fists. He struggles to get hold of himself, and finally throws himself into Laura's arms.

"I'm eleven years old," Antoine begins. "Lying in a cot, shivering from terror and loneliness. The bedroom is tiny, but Bérin has set up a whole bookshelf for me, full of books he picks up at stands in the street. One of those books I've never given away, a science textbook. On the cover, a gigantic Tyrannosaurus, its mouth wide open, threatening. For me, that image is Rosa. In the evening, there was no electricity. They said that the hordes of jackals, hyenas, two-legged dogs, wild boars, and leopards would take advantage of the darkness, emerge from their dens to kill their victims. I imagined an army of animals, teeth bared. Leading them, Rosa, just like the Tyrannosaurus. Me, I'm just waiting for the chance to cut off her head."

Laura and Antoine are filled with dread as the past carries them away, uncertain if their nightmare will ever end. For them, there's no more daily routine, no day, no night. Within them, irreparable destruction; all those memories, sometimes twisted, sometimes intact, relentless waves of grimacing shadows flood through their bodies. They no longer know how to live with the sadness; they are drained by the unbearable pain that surges each time they evoke their shattered childhoods. The atmosphere between them grows so heavy that some days they just avoid each other. Exhausted, Laura retreats to the bedroom where Antoine led her the day she finally came to the big house. She sleeps the day away, while Antoine mechanically cares for Rosa. Still under the shock of Janice's testimony, stunned by Laura's tales and the despair that ravaged her childhood, Antoine feels something give way, a profound shift in the very core of his being.

20

Three weeks of agony. Three long weeks had passed since Antoine and Laura last spoke. While she wages a merciless war against the memories pushing her to make a clean break, Antoine continues his attacks on Rosa. His voice now conveys an infinite sadness; he seems to have run through all his reserves of anger. He barely eats anymore. He's abandoned the tall stool on which he perched, looming over his adversary, in favor of the small folding cot. Leaning back, like her, on a pile of cushions, he continues his indictment, telling, explaining, questioning, but mostly writing and correcting. The floodgates of his heart have burst open. An enormous breach, too big to patch, has opened up, and through it flow those images gleaned from the archives buried in the entrails of this "country of unmemory," as he calls their island. Laura's silence worries him. He's champing at the bit, and his will to live is unable to deaden his pain.

One night, Laura wakes up with a start. She begins frantically digging back down through the tunnel to her childhood in that school for young girls: the accents of the nuns, those ghosts with diaphanous hands, come back to her. With eyes full of compassion, in muffled voices, they all said, "Pray, our children, pray again and again." The girls were taught to recite long prayers that they didn't understand. "Our Father, who art in Heaven, forgive us our trespasses ..." But her father was nowhere to be found, and of what trespasses was she guilty? Like icy water falling drip by drip into her heart, those long lists of all the saints she needed to beg for forgiveness came back to her. What sins could she have committed to deserve ending up in Rosa's house? As a child, she put her whole soul into those prayers, hoping some miracle would bring her parents back. You have to believe in miracles, that's what Julienne taught her.

That very night, Laura kneels by her bed, as she used to do with Julienne. How can we understand life's torments? she wonders. Understand what is beyond us, know what is beyond our ken? How to understand the incomprehensible, the madness that kept making me lose control of time? In that moment, when Laura feels so small, from the furthest reaches of herself comes a prayer whispered in her ear, it seems, by Julienne: "Lord God," she says "finally ... I give this all back to you. Today, I have to choose sides!"

At breakfast, Antoine finds her broken, with large circles under her eyes, her face distraught. Another sleepless night. She quickly swallows down her coffee.

"I'm going back to the village," she announces as she stands, without finishing her breakfast.

Antoine gives a start and puts down his cup.

"You're still afraid I'm going to run away, is that it? In the end, you're right to."

Laura's words bear the stamp of her usual mix of irony and bitterness.

"It's time for us to move on to the next stage," she continues. "We have to finish the job. I can't take it anymore. What if we leave Gourdaix, even just for one day? That would certainly give us some perspective, let's really see what options we have."

"I'm sorry I panicked," Antoine confesses. "It was a reflex. Really, your idea is excellent. We should get an early start. How about eight o'clock tomorrow?"

"Yes, we're on for eight!"

Back home, Laura goes through each room. She looks around sadly, running a hesitant hand along the walls, the paint faded in places where pictures, photos used to hang—she'd taken them all down. The closets are half empty. She spends the day sorting, throwing things out, destroying much of it.

While she's focused on that task, Antoine tears apart Rosa's famous desk on the upper floor. He finds a whole stash of documents that he scans, a look of disbelief and consternation on his face. Why had Rosa brought them all to France? Why didn't she just destroy them? He holds in his hand an impressive list of all those who disappeared in the famous Fort-Dimanche prison, piles of death certificates signed by doctors who served as morticians on the regime's payroll. Notices of sentences, execution orders, too many to count. But there is one bundle of papers that matters the most: execution orders signed by Rosa Bosquet, including this one: "Order number 476, Guibert residence, rue des Hortensias." 476, 476. As Antoine repeats those numbers, he feels them hammering on his skull, stabbing into him like a spear. That incessant tick-tock hounds him, 476: three numbers, his memory's eternal refrain.

His discovery, in that same desk, of a series of six drawers with fake bottoms, crammed full of banknotes in high denominations, doesn't surprise him. Duvalier's dignitaries made a habit of burying huge sums of money in their gardens, under blocks of cement, that they'd dig up just before fleeing the country. They couldn't put them in a bank, even though they knew bankers always turned a blind eye.

The next morning, when Laura's sedan pulls up at the bottom of the hill, Antoine is ready to go. He reaches through the open window. She grasps his hand and invites him to sit down beside her.

"Hello, Laura."

She doesn't answer right away. She's scanning Antoine's face for signs, hints, unsure of what she's hoping to find.

"Hello, Antoine," she finally replies, as she pulls out onto the road.

She'd like to keep her eyes peeled on the winding road, but she steals glances now and again at Antoine, who's still humming that tune he'd made Rosa listen to one whole day long.

"Please, Antoine," begs Laura, irritated.

"Why so glum, Laura? You look like you're going to a funeral. We'll see the end of this tunnel soon."

Laura doesn't answer. Once again, she's retreated behind the walls of her fortress. The trees and signs stream by. The sky is a triumphant blue, the road, a long, impassive river of grey. The car weaves along. Holding tight to the steering wheel, Laura hits the gas. Worried, Antoine coughs, then starts to tap his fingers nervously on the car door and whistle. It would just take one little thing, he thinks, life is holding on by a string. Just one little thing, a moment of madness … The twists and turns of the road become more worrisome. Antoine's mind is racing: how can he stop thinking that all it would take is a little swerve to send us to our deaths, right then and there, leaving Rosa behind? He stifles a shiver, and, hoping to make Laura slow down, he says:

"Do you know, Laura, that even long after her move here, Rosa kept receiving dividends from the traffic in blood and organs? I found documents about that in her desk. That trade was organized back in the county by someone named Lucien Cambrona."

"I thought as much," Laura replies. "Rosa was the head of an association for the adoption of orphans, they'd given it a crazy name, *Cœur de Gazelle*. Who knows what happened to those kids after they were supposedly adopted. To think I could have ended up scattered in pieces, a kidney here, an eye over there, sold to the highest bidder."

"Dictatorships are good for that, too."

"Even when faced with rock-solid evidence, it's hard to take it all in," Laura murmurs.

She closes her eyes for a brief instant and the car skids.

"It's thanks to the money from the trade in organs and blood, and from the sale of children, that Rosa became rich. But that will remain a secret if we don't act, Laura. The banks will never betray her; the banks are real catacombs."

Laura's teeth start chattering so hard she decides to pull over. On the verge of a nervous breakdown, she stops on the side of the road and lets her head fall onto the steering wheel. A look of terror flashes across her eyes as she lifts her head and says:

"But what are we going to do? I still don't see where to start. I've made one decision, though, I'm leaving Gourdaix. Once and for all. Where will I find safe harbor? I have no idea. But ... there's something else."

The pause that follows seems endless to Antoine. Fearing what may come, he watches her lower her head once more. She cracks her fingers so loudly that Antoine grabs her hands. They're so clammy, he freezes.

"Laura, what it is?"

"I have to tell you ..." she murmurs, but then falls silent again.

And in a horrible flash, Antoine understands and shouts:

"Rosa put all her money in your name!"

"All of it."

"I figured as much. But I think you shouldn't give too much weight to that, or rather, you need to make a distinction between what it represents and how much of it there is.

Stunned, Laura stares at him.

"Try to understand," he tries to explain. "The importance of all that money comes primarily from the fact that it was amassed in ways and in circumstances we know quite well. It's blood money, money for pain and horror. That means there's an ethical question to consider, for sure. But that's for you alone to decide, Laura. Now, we have to focus on what's most urgent: What are we going to do with Rosa?"

"The easiest thing would be for both of us to just go away, leave her there alone in her bed. Fire Marie, shut the doors and windows, abandon her, just like she did when she threw people into cellars and prisons."

"I've thought of that. But sometime or another, someone would find her, and the authorities would start searching for you. Don't forget, Laura, you are tied to Rosa. Me," Antoine adds, "I dream of throwing her off a cliff, there are so many around here. She'd never be found. The wolves would devour her. I imagine them sinking their fangs into her flesh."

"I'm going to faint if you keep going."

She stretches up to look at her face in the rearview mirror.

"We look like two lunatics."

"You just don't get it," Antoine concedes, his eyes glistening.

He grabs her arm; his fingers are on fire. Exhausted, he finally lets himself sink back against the seat. He closes his eyes for an instant, then sits bolt upright.

"Why don't we set the house on fire?"

Terrified, Laura just stares.

"You're losing your mind, Antoine," she whispers. "Just think, all those trees, imagine the blaze, the dense vegetation … You don't know what you're saying."

"Thank you for bringing me back to reality," Antoine mumbles.

He gives a long sigh. Once again, there they are, two exiles, each alone in their suffering.

To Laura's mind, despite his strength and his clear-eyed analysis, Antoine tends to fall back on a superficial, romantic vision of things. She can't do the same. Birds float high above in a hypnotic ballet. Laura watches them, telling herself that she'll always be a prisoner, a prisoner to pain, to fear. The chirping of the birds, the rustling of the wind, everything seems to remind her of that impossible dream of freedom.

"There's one thing you'll never understand."

Antoine's voice swells up; quiet at first, it grows in strength as his tale progresses.

"All my life, I've watched those I love disappear. Each morning, I open my eyes and see the same thing, a house collapsing; my daily hallucination, it's maddening. It rises up there in front of me, and I'm under assault from the cries and the howls. That's it, Laura, the loss, the irreparable loss that I experience each and every day that God brings, a loss that makes everything, including my own life, meaningless. I am eternally lost, Laura, because of what was taken from me, what no longer exists but is always so present. Maybe that's what's different between us. You, you built an abstract universe for yourself, you evoke memories that seem to have absolutely no hold on you. It's not a criticism, far from it. I'm talking about a kind of peace I'll never know. Rosa not only took from me those I loved, she stole my very life, the peace of my soul. She killed me, do you understand?"

Antoine's inflections are indescribable, his words seem almost perfect, Laura thinks. That idea plunges her into an undefinable state of confusion, for she has no idea what to say, even as the same questions circle around and around endlessly in her head, in her troubled mind: How long will it take? How many years do we need to overcome pain? Will there ever be a day when the only thing you want is to forget? When, out of strength and ammunition, you just have to give up the fight? She'd like to find the courage to tell him all that, but she's never had any confidence in herself, has always believed she was incapable of thinking for herself: "I'm just a branch, torn down by a wild wind," Laura muses, "a branch deported, far from any familiar landmarks, with no future."

"I think at some point I just gave up," she tries to explain. "Measured against pain, everything else seems laughable, Antoine, really. So, I made a choice, I think, to give up, to give up on myself. Or, if you prefer, I took a shortcut, a sideroad."

"I can't let myself give up, Laura. Hunting down Rosa, making her pay—that's always been my only goal in life, do you see? We have to hold her accountable, make her suffer."

"But you say it yourself, nothing will ease your pain. We have no choice but to turn her over to the authorities," Laura declares, sounding unsure of herself. "Didn't you say you have a file?"

"Quite a thick one, to say the least. But, there we'd run a big risk."

"What risk?"

"Think about that charade, for example, the Pinochet affair, or think about Barbie, or Aussaresses, who even went so far as to write a book justifying his criminal acts. And what to say about all those generals, from Chile, Argentina, Uruguay, those soldiers and paramilitary who were never held accountable, from Guatemala, Paraguay, El Salvador, and who knows where else? And let's not forget those who taught the art of torture in that famous School of the Americas! It's a long list, Laura. Those assassins are protected."

"But," Laura pleads again, "there are judges who bring them to justice ... I've read that some judges expand the scope of their authority to include international law just so they can try some of these criminals. That's what happened when Pinochet was arrested in England, on a warrant from a Spanish judge, for crimes committed in Chile. There's also a law in Belgium that allows them to try people for crimes against humanity."

Antoine interrupts her.

"Yes, but are they ever convicted? Today, leaders accept, justify, and legalize torture in the name of the war on terror. Torture, it seems, is only a crime if there's an intent to cause suffering. No intention, no torture! There you have it! In the end, if we call upon international justice, we risk running up against a system where the odds are stacked in favor of the assassins."

"So, you're saying any old lawyer could claim that this woman, who spent her whole life deliberately inventing ways to make people suffer, who killed and ordered the deaths of so many people, did so without any intention of committing torture?"

"It wouldn't be the first time. But I haven't been fighting all this time to end up with a result that would be just one more insult to my family," Antoine thunders. "I don't give a damn about slogans—they're just diversions used to spare the guilty. I live by one word alone: Justice!"

Out of control, Antoine shouts at Laura, who gnaws on her fists, huddled against the door.

"If it can help you to understand, think of me as an addict. I need justice, like a druggie needs a fix."

Antoine's hands are actually twitching and his lips twist into a sneer.

"I need this, Laura, do you understand, so that I can keep my eyes open, continue moving ahead. I must see Rosa Bosquet suffer. I have to. Rosa must pay!"

The words Antoine had repressed for so long come out in a gut-wrenching rush. Listening to him, Laura's face is twisted by pain.

"We'll have to punish Rosa ourselves," he concludes, his voice suddenly like ice.

Laura starts the car up again. Antoine's last words hit her like a rockslide, an avalanche that buries her. Walled up in his loss and in his quest, Antoine has simply abandoned me by the side of the road, she tells herself. I'll never be able to reach him, never. Solitude assails her. She realizes she has no will of her own, no soul. Antoine has just reminded her of that. Her soul was stolen from her by the *reines-choches*: she is nothing, lost for all eternity. She has nothing, nothing but a junk box in which she's shoved all of her memories pell-mell and that she opens from time to time to pull out random bits of her past. Now she scatters them along the ribbon of road: bits of conversations and mysteries, Julienne's sighs, her unbelievable stories, Rosa's hardened face, the parties she dragged her to, the bedroom with blue curtains. Just when did I get lost, Laura wonders, mumbling softly to herself, as if she were alone. She drives on in a trance, like a robot, following her reflexes. Beside her, Antoine seems to be crying. Laura does her best to avoid catching his eyes. He, too, will find his place in that box with all the other junk.

21

It's almost night when they return. They climb the stairs. The voice of Irène Papas—warm, enveloping, Antoine thinks, too beautiful for an alligator's ears—intones for the umpteenth time her hymn to liberty. Going into the room, Laura observes Rosa as if seeing her for the first time. Here, she tells herself, there's no clear line between human and animal. Rosa's fingers are, as always, still covered with rings; they grip the mauve blanket she pulls up tight around her. The night before, Antoine had put on her head a ridiculous bonnet he'd dug up who knows where. It has a ruffle of white lace and the strips of ribbon used to tie it on are lost in the mass of greyish flesh beneath her chin. She reminds Laura of Columbine, that cheeky maid in old plays. The curtain has finally fallen for you, Rosa, she thinks. She'd like to be able to laugh, laugh at that face, so pathetic today, laugh thinking that just a few years before, Rosa Bosquet was a powerful woman who made a whole country tremble. In those days, she wasn't ugly; quite the contrary, people said she was beautiful. Like so many other ignoramuses of her ilk, she was obsessed by her light skin and smooth hair, which she often wore combed to frame her face, highlighting the imperturbable brow, symbol of her omnipotence. Where had that woman gone, the one who wore stiletto heels, thigh-high boots, and shoes with pointed toes like bird beaks? Dead, swallowed up by time. That Rosa Bosquet, Laura tells herself, no longer exists. She died along with the Supreme Leader. All that's left in this room is a mass of rotting flesh. Laura knows full well that this has nothing to do with age but rather results from the poison filtering out through Rosa's pores; that corrosive liquid, the venom distilled by the Supreme Leader, made its way through her veins to drown everything right up to her soul.

Standing before that immense bed, facing those pitiful remains, Laura feels an uncertain anguish. In a television documentary, they showed some of those people, who used to be men and women, now robbed of all dignity, fed as if on a production line, one spoonful to the left, another to the right. The same dull eyes, the same gaping mouth waiting for the next spoonful. A bath every two weeks, one relative complained. The nurses showed no restraint that day, even though strangers were there filming—manhandling them and shouting, as if they were cowherds, Laura recalls. Some of the frightened old folks grimaced, thinking no doubt about a remnant of splendor hidden somewhere within them. Soon Rosa will join one of these flocks on the last leg of life's journey, she tells herself, as she turns to look at Antoine. Aware of the painful emotions boiling up in Laura, Antoine remains silent. He just stopped the record.

Angry at having been left all alone and to have missed her midday meal, Rosa rolls her beastly eyes and growls hoarsely: "Houououuuunnn! Houuuuuun!"

"Grumble as much as you like, you old bag," Antoine mumbles, then he quickly grabs one of the notebooks lying on the bedside table.

He tears out a page and starts writing: "I, Rosa Bosquet, born in Rivère Chaudières, in the commune of Sialaberim, in the year 1936, admit to having been the *Reine-Choche*, a *Fillette Lalo*, a demon, leader of the death squads known as the National Security Volunteers, during the reign of the tyrant Duvalier. I also admit ordering the assassination of ..." There he stops, pen in air, his mind elsewhere.

"What is it?" Laura asks.

"How many deaths does Rosa have on her conscience?"

"What does the number matter," Laura replies. "One death, that's already a lot, one death, a single death, that's already too many. But what do you plan to do with what you're writing?"

"Make Rosa sign it."

"Why? What good will that do?"

"Truth be told, I have no idea. But I need this paper, I need this confession, I need it."

"And just how do you think you're going to make her sign it?"

"That remains to be seen," he replies, dead serious. "Let me finish writing: 'I, Rosa Bosquet, I admit ...'" he reads aloud.

"Houuuuuuun!"

"You'll have no choice but to sign, Rosa! Whether you want to or not, you will sign this."

He waves the paper beneath Rosa's whiskery chin.

"No rifle, no bayonet, but you will sign," Antoine declares, with great dignity.

"Houuuuuuuuuuuuun! Houuuuuuuuuuuuuuuuuun! Houuuuuuuuuuuuuuuuuuun!"

Laura plugs her ears. She can't bear this fight anymore. Suddenly, a brilliant idea pops into her head; she moves toward Antoine, whispers in his ear. Antoine seems to agree. She leaves the room. Antoine has placed the pen and paper on the floor. Rosa's eyes go from the door Laura left open to Antoine, then to the paper, a bright splotch, a square of light visible on the ground as shadows grow in the room.

A light clinking, the sounds of dishes and steps as Laura returns, carrying a tray laden with food: half a cold chicken, mashed potatoes, salad. Rosa starts to wriggle.

"Wonderful!" says Antoine, taking hold of the tray. "Now," he announces, his voice triumphant, "it's between us two, Rosa Bosquet! You sign, I put the tray down in front of you, and I'll even go get you a second serving if that's what you want. Otherwise, I eat it all and give you just the bones to gnaw on, the empty plates to lick."

Rosa's whiskery chin recoils in pain, her fingers stiffen and reach toward the piece of paper that waits impassively on the floor. Antoine rolls the table toward the bed, places the paper on it, grabs Rosa's hand and slips a pen between her fingers. At the bottom of the page, the eleven misaligned letters take shape, an angular and shaky script. Without a word, Antoine picks up the paper and places the tray in front of Rosa. She grabs the chicken and swallows it down in a fraction of a second.

Caught up in the spectacle of Rosa's gluttony, Laura doesn't notice that Antoine has left the room. She screams in horror, her heart jumping out of her chest, when he comes back carrying the display case with the twenty-four knives. Realizing he'd torn it off the wall, she's too stunned to speak. The blades shimmer, the screws are still sunk in the wood. With bloodshot eyes and trembling shoulders, Antoine advances.

Laura feels the ground give way beneath her, she sways but finds the strength to run off down the long hallway. She starts to vomit before reaching a bathroom. Terrorized, she stands up, slips and falls again, flat out in her own vomit. In a stupor, she stumbles to her feet and stares at her hands, covered in phlegm. She shouts like never before in her life when she hears Rosa trumpeting. Antoine, she tells herself, is fighting for his life, and me, I'm off in the shadows, more alone than ever, friendless and abandoned, once again. I've just lost him for good.

Three months later, sitting on the veranda of the little house with blue shutters, the house she has long forced herself to love, in the same rattan rocker as on the day she welcomed Antoine and things took a decisive turn, Laura tries to make sense of it all. Suitcases, zippered and locked, wait in the kitchen, the real estate agent will be there in less than an hour. Laura struggles as best she can to banish from her mind that image of Rosa perched in her wheelchair. Rosa had always refused to use that chair, which was lying in a closet. How she tries to impose her will, to resist. Antoine insisted on leaving the cap from her days as a *reine-choche* on her head. Rosa tugs on the cap and drags along the mauve blanket that she refuses to give up. All the way to Nice, where they had finally managed to find the most lugubrious of hospices, Rosa bellows, like a dying whale.

Filled with disgust, Laura recalls the face of the man who introduced himself as the manager of the establishment. His eyes still heavy with sleep, although it was almost noon, his hair sticking up all over, he tucked the tails of a grimy shirt into his rumpled trousers. All the red scaly skin on his forehead, peeling off in little flakes that were scattered over his clothes. But the almost open look in his eyes when he glanced at Rosa, all scrunched up in her chair, seemed to give the woman a glimmer of hope. She stopped bellowing. She was trying, one might say, to win over that man, in hopes of improving her daily lot in this hellish place. Pricking their ears, Laura and Antoine could hear groans, snores, sobs, and moaning coming from the floor above, and, in the midst of it all, a surly voice demanding silence. Outside the window, the garden looked like a battlefield. A couple, a man and a woman, walked stiffly in starched dignity, the man pulling along the woman who was tottering on her legs, two thick sticks swathed in stockings the color of mourning. Like a capricious coquette, the woman held out her hands, whimpered, begged for a rose, which was surrounded by a tangle of thorns on a fence covered with jagged barbed wire. Her face as white as a clown's, she trembled.

"That mad woman thinks she's an old countess," the manager explained with a smile. "We have several cases like that here. She introduces herself as the Countess of Roquefront and repeats every day that she was richer than all the Rockefellers and the Onassises combined, and lost it all gambling. She had, so she says, her own personal suite at the grand casino in Monte-Carlo."

Her eyes fixed on her rings, which are worth a fortune, Rosa listened. Laura was sure she was trying to figure out how to cash in those gaudy bits of metal.

They went over the forms they'd already filled out, describing Rosa as an old acquaintance with no family in France. Family name: Bosquet Alligator; given name: Rosa. Particular traits: she no longer speaks.

"The result of a heart attack?" the man asked.

"Precisely," Antoine acknowledged.

"One more for the list," was the manager's only comment.

Her heart pounding, her hands clammy, Laura signed the paperwork and gave instructions so the establishment could make withdrawals to pay for Rosa's care. The man folded the mauve blanket and placed it on Rosa's knees.

"If you'd like, you can follow me and see where she'll be staying," the man proposed, as he slid the final documents into a drawer.

The wheelchair squeaked and bumped along the hallway's dirty, uneven tiles. The scent of bleach and urine pursued them. A room with grimy walls, patches of peeling plaster. In the back, a curtain of faded blue, torn in multiple places, divided the space in two. A row of metal beds, six pairs of eyes on one side, six on the other—twenty-four in total—assessed the new arrivals, staring at them greedily.

They went through the dining room. A nauseating smell of wet mop, grease, and bleach. Even the coffee, which usually smells so inviting, had a strange and unpleasant odor. In a corner, a television set. A small group of elderly residents, like shadows in rocking chairs, nursed the past while sucking on their soft gums.

Laura looked at them, a hand clapped over her mouth. She had just realized that they were all tied to their chairs, by their wrists or their ankles.

"It's the only way to control them," the manager explained. "Otherwise, they risk falling and breaking their bones. I don't understand why they always want to watch the news; some make quite a fuss if they miss it. It seems to comfort them to see the world falling apart, just like them," he quipped.

Laura wanted to flee. In desperation, she grabbed hold of Antoine's arm. One woman, seated in front of a deck of cards, was playing by herself, her deformed mouth twisted into a smile. Another, who was smearing lipstick all over her chin, was reprimanded sternly by an attendant, and started to moan.

Antoine and Laura stayed only long enough to realize that they would carry those images away with them, stored alongside all the others accumulated over the course of their lives: the burning house, collapsing walls, flames licking up over the molten metal; Sister Emmanuelle and her white veil, tears in her crystal eyes; Julienne and Maman dlo; and the faces they could only barely recall of their parents. In silence, they retraced their steps up the hallway. When I get back to the house, Laura told herself, I'll have to burn the clothes I'm wearing, along with the shoes and everything else, even the purse. She'll shut up the bunker and the blue house; then she'll leave, go anywhere, to the farthest ends of the world.

Further down the hall, in front of another television set, people sit at a table and eat. They're broadcasting images from a distant war. Houses collapsing under missile fire, women kneeling with arms outstretched, wailing. On a makeshift bed, naked as worm, a child. He's maybe ten years old, Antoine said. With burns all over his body and no more arms. The image faded away, or rather bled into another: more houses, another far-off corner of the world. Men, women, children, picked up and carried away, pools of blood. Yet another image: an island, in the distance, the sea and a port, piles of garbage, people slogging through the mud alongside pigs. A few meters away, a group of young men armed with machetes and rifles, shouting as they surround a haggard man. All around, onlookers are waiting … waiting for what? With the sharp points of their weapons, the young men trace a skull on the neck of the condemned man. Those judges were twelve, maybe thirteen, and they're afraid of nothing, no matter how horrible.

"It must be a documentary on child-soldiers," Antoine murmured.

"Maybe from Rwanda, Chad, or Congo," Laura replied. "But I almost think its Haiti."

"You're right. It looks like Haiti."

Despite themselves, horror kept them imprisoned there longer than they would have liked, surrounded by that smell of old flesh. They were paralyzed by it.

The Listerine smile and perfectly coiffed hair of the newscaster announcing the next image: Palestine. The Israeli soldier looks like a Palestinian, Laura remarked. He's maybe twenty, maybe less. Perched on a tank, he stares, as if he were in a theater, at an old woman, clasping onto a tree, an olive tree. The last remaining vestige of what had been her life, a witness to the place where her house once stood. All that was left was a tree, its silvery leaves obscured by the grey smoke from the remains of the house, its ashes still smoldering.

Saint-Laurent du Maroni
French Guyana, May 2003

Sant'Agata Bolognese
Alberghi Divina Commedia
Italy, August 2007

Afterword: 2024

The original French version of *Un alligator nommé Rosa* was published in Montreal in 2007 by Les Éditions du remue-ménage. My acknowledgments for that original edition, combining creative writing and commemoration, allowed me to honor women and men who, in the tradition of uncompromising anti-Duvalierism, had entrusted their precious memory to me. From them I inherited principles that allow us to say loudly and clearly an unambiguous "No" to a universe based on brute force and controlled by a small, privileged minority—by which I mean, the predators who have held Haiti in their talons since the Duvalier era.

Several years later, during a return visit to my native land, I was invited by the Alliance Française of Jacmel to speak to a group comprised primarily of high school students. Several of them raised questions about the lack of any serious attention to memories of the Duvalier era. They had no access, they said, to the collective memory, the historical memory of that period. The extent of their frustration was palpable; they felt like they'd been had, taken advantage of. Just who was benefiting from that silence? they seemed to wonder.

On January 16, 2011, we witnessed an awful, scandalous, and truly unimaginable event. A crowd of mostly young people—confused, no doubt, but really searching for something to hold onto besides the "*macoutisme*" that continues to fester as it destroys any hope for change—rushed to the airport to greet and cheer on Jean-Claude Duvalier, who, unlike du Bellay's Ulysses, had returned to the scene of his crimes, "lacking in common sense and guided by folly," hoping to "live out his days" in the place he considered his fiefdom, his Duvalierist nest once again feathered with a new brood. What about the respect due the thousands of victims of the Duvalier regime? And just who are those victims, really? Sadly, the young people of Haiti know all too little about the Duvaliers' destructive fury, about the thousands who died or disappeared, the decimated generation of the 1960s, or about all those crimes that so many, including first-hand witnesses, are determined to erase. In this moment when we see so much backtracking around the world, our vigilance—and let's say it openly and without hesitation, our memory work—has never been more essential.

The theme of this novel is upsetting to many people, although, truth be told, it gives only a brief glimpse into the evil deeds of just one of the torturers who served the elder Duvalier, Papa Doc. They certainly know full well what bothers them about it—and I suspect they have given some thought to the sources of their unease. As for the memory work, we hope that this is just a beginning, because we must say, again and again, an enthusiastic "Yes" to life as we battle on for the preservation of historical memory, which is the essence of life. We must uphold our duty to memory and refuse to let our society be kept hostage by the unholy beasts who depend, above all, on the complicity of some and the indifference of others.

Duty to memory? Essential! We must say no to the Duvalierist shadows that swallow up our valiant people, and lift up a shield capable of protecting memory from systematic erasure by those who deliberately opt for indifference and lies.

Duty to memory? Indispensable, because we must never lose sight of the fact that, if forgetting is necessary to "move on to something else," as we are so often told, an "excess of forgetfulness" is so much more dangerous. Forgetfulness is nothing other than the abyss of annihilation!

The publication of this English translation of *Rosa the Alligator* is the fruit of the determination of two women: professors Amy Reid and Joëlle Vitiello. Amy Reid, an exceptional translator, was so horrified by the unbearable brutality of the Duvalier regime depicted in the novel that she knew it needed to be translated to reach a larger readership, and so dedicated herself to this work, heart and soul. I owe her many thanks for her careful translation and for her efforts to find the right publisher for the project. My thanks, too, to Florida State University and Liverpool University Press for publishing it.

My heartfelt thanks to Joëlle Vitiello, a specialist in Haitian literature. She was a constant support to Amy in her work, reading and editing the translation, and providing an insightful introduction to the novel.

Finally, I must also underscore the important work undertaken by the Fondation Devoir de Mémoire in Haiti. In a context of endless and daily struggles, in a most challenging environment, its members must reach deep within themselves to find the strength, strategies, and courage to fulfill their mission, the duty to memory that they have taken on as their own. Their valor is a true source of inspiration.

Marie-Célie Agnant
Montreal, 2024

www.ingramcontent.com/pod-product-compliance
Lightning Source LLC
Chambersburg PA
CBHW020030160126

38357CB00012B/248